AT
WILLIE TUCKER'S
PLACE

AT WILLIE TUCKER'S PLACE

ALISON MORGAN

Illustrated by Trevor Stubley

THOMAS NELSON INC., PUBLISHERS

Nashville, Tennessee / New York, New York

No character in this book is intended to represent any actual person; all the incidents of the story are entirely fictional in nature.

Text Copyright © 1975 by Alison Morgan
Illustrations Copyright © 1975 by Trevor Stubley

First U.S. edition

Library of Congress Cataloging in Publication Data

Morgan, Alison
  At Willie Tucker's place.

  Summary: Visiting Willie Tucker who lives next door to an army training area proves to be a dangerous adventure for ten-year-old Dan.
  I. Stubley, Trevor.   II. Title.
PZ7.M8202At3   [Fic]   76–41183
ISBN 0–8407–6515–0

For Hugh

Contents

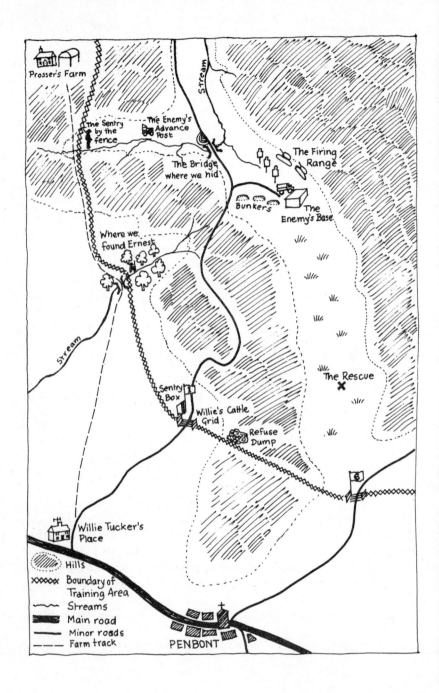

1
Dan Goes on a Visit

"Willie *Tucker?*" said Jimmy. "What on earth do you want to go and stay with him for?"

"I just do," said Dan. He bent over the picture he was drawing of a battle scene, and colored in spurts of red from the wheeling airplanes and from the muzzles of the antiaircraft guns.

"I think you're nuts," said Jean. "He's so *dull.*"

Dan looked at her for a moment, then returned to his picture. The lower half of the page was pretty well covered with soldiers, all very small and pinlike, manning guns, driving tanks, sniping from behind bunkers, or lying dead on the ground. The ones in gray uniforms were the bad guys, and it was mostly those who were dead; the good guys were in green because Dan didn't have a khaki-colored crayon.

One green figure was much bigger than the others, and was standing on a hilltop giving orders. Dan crooked his arm around that part of the paper, to shield it from the prying eyes of his elder brother and sister. He carefully wrote "Capt. Daniel Price" in tiny letters underneath.

Jimmy was fifteen and Jean thirteen. Dan, who was almost eleven, wished they did not always think they knew what was best for him.

His father was in the kitchen, drying his hands on the towel behind the door, and had overheard the last part of the conversation.

"Who's so dull?" he asked, coming into the room in his socks, and settling himself in the old armchair by the fireplace while he shuffled into his slippers. Mr. Price was a farmer in the Welsh hills, and he had been out trimming hedges all day.

"Willie Tucker," said Jimmy. "You know, Dan's friend, who keeps coming here to stay."

"Dan wants to go and stay with *him,*" said Jean.

"What's the matter with staying with us, then, Dan?" asked his father.

"Nothing," said Dan, glancing up to make sure his father was joking, not insulted. "Why shouldn't I go and stay with Willie?"

"No reason at all," said Mr. Price, "only you'll have to get Auntie Ceinwen to ask you."

"He's done that," said Jean. "You know when he wanted you to take Biddy to compete in the sheep-dog trials, and you wouldn't . . ."

"Biddy wasn't old enough."

"I know, so Dan went and asked Mr. Williams if he could go with him to help look after his dog . . ."

"I know," said Mr. Price. "I noticed our Dan had leave of absence all day today. Did you have a good time, Dan?"

"Yep," said Dan. "Mr. Williams' dog, Moss, won the cup."

"He always does," said Jimmy.

"Lately, he has," said Mr. Price. "But do you remember our old Lady? She won here in Llanwern a couple of times, must be a few years back now. Biddy's her granddaughter, and very like her, very like her."

"I wish you'd entered her today, Dad," said Jimmy.

"No, no, she's too young to take around, but I think maybe I'll try her out at the trials here in three week's time; she won't do much good but it'll be experience for her."

"The point is," said Jean, sticking to her story, "the only

reason why Dan wanted to go to the Penbont sheep-dog trials was because he knew Auntie Ceinwen would be there, with Willie, and he could ask her if he could go and stay."

"What did she say, Dan?"

For answer, Dan unraveled a crumpled piece of paper and laid it on the table in front of his father. He read, "Can Dan come on Monday the twelfth and stay for a week? Yours truly, Ceinwen Tucker."

"Has your mother seen this?" Mr. Price asked.

"Yes," said Dan. "She says I can go if you can take me."

"As it happens," said his father, "it's cattle market at Penbont that Monday, and I was thinking of taking a few ewes in the back of the van."

"I know," said Dan.

"Trust Dan," said Jimmy.

"I *did* know. I heard Dad talking about it a few days ago."

"Got it all worked out, haven't you?" said Mr. Price. He glanced at the sheet of paper in his hand. "It was lucky Auntie Ceinwen took her writing paper with her to the trials, wasn't it?"

Dan bent over his picture and said nothing.

Jean, seeing the grin on her father's face, took a closer look at the note. "She uses the same paper as us, too. Dan?"

"Uh-uh."

"You didn't write this yourself, did you?"

Dan looked up then, really surprised, but his father answered for him. "No, of course he didn't. He just thought if Auntie Ceinwen didn't write then and there, she'd never get around to it, so he took pen and paper all ready. That's right, isn't it, Dan?"

Dan felt relieved. He was shocked that Jean should have suspected him of such a low-down trick, which, to be fair, had never entered his head. "Well, you know what Auntie Ceinwen is," he said.

They all did know. Willie's mother was not a true aunt, but

some sort of cousin of the Prices. She lived about twelve miles away with her two daughters—Shirley, who had just left school and started work, Marie, who was fourteen—and Willie, who was ten. Her husband had died about the time Willie was born. The Prices had never seen very much of their cousins, except when they all happened to meet at something like the sheep-dog trials, but about a year ago Dan had spent an afternoon alone with Willie, when both their mothers had gone to visit a mutual friend in the hospital and the two boys had been told to amuse themselves in the hospital grounds. That was when Dan discovered that Willie lived on the fringe of an army firing range up in the hills.

"What happens there?" asked Dan.

"I don't know. They fire guns and all that."

"At people?"

"No, at targets."

"What sort of targets?"

"I don't know. Old tanks and such."

"How do they get them up there?"

"Oh, a lot of stuff goes up the lane past our house."

"Real tanks?"

"I don't know. Lots of trucks and things. Makes the TV go all funny."

Dan couldn't think why anyone would be watching television when army convoys were passing the front door, but though he questioned Willie eagerly about everything he could think of, he got very little real information out of him.

After that, he kept on asking his mother if Willie could come and stay for part of each vacation, and Willie had spent a week at the farm later that summer, and had also stayed at Christmas, and at Easter. Each time, Dan tried to learn more about the army training area, telling Willie the kind of things he wanted to know, and asking him to find the answers before the next visit. Willie never refused, but he never did anything about it, either. He just forgot, or thought it wasn't important.

To Dan it was very important. Every time he settled down to draw another army battle scene, with Captain Daniel Price directing operations from a corner of the page, there were a lot of details he couldn't be sure about. He collected all the pictures and magazines he could get hold of and spent all his pocket money on little plastic soldiers and watched all the army films on television, but none of it was the same as seeing the real thing. More and more, he grew determined to get himself to the scene of action.

The rest of Dan's family were puzzled by his sudden friendship with such a dull boy as Willie Tucker, because whatever faults they might find with Dan, and frequently did, dullness was not one of them. But though Dan was willing enough to chatter away about almost anything under the sun, he never told any of his family about why he wanted to stay with Willie. They knew, of course, that he was always inventing army battle scenes, and teased him about it sometimes. Dan was used to that. But this ambition to see the real-live army at work—that was something private, and special. Only Willie knew about that, and Willie was so thick, it didn't matter.

Just over a week later, Dan stood looking out over the training area. He had been at the Tuckers' house for less than two hours.

Auntie Ceinwen had been surprised when Dan suggested going for a walk with Willie as soon as they had had their tea. "Don't you want to watch television?" she said. "Shirl and Marie never miss 'Crossroads.'"

"Nor do you, Mom," said Shirley, slumped in a chair after a long day at the shop.

"Does Willie watch it?" asked Dan, surprised.

"I don't know," said Auntie Ceinwen. It was something she had never thought about.

"Nope," said Willie.

"What do you do, then?" asked Dan.

"Nothing much." It was a typical Willie remark.

"Can we go for a walk?"

"I don't mind." Willie never minded anything. It used to irritate Jimmy and Jean when Willie stayed at the farm, but Dan had discovered that to have a friend who could never make up his mind about anything was very convenient for someone like himself, who had no trouble at all in always knowing what he wanted to do.

"Right," said Dan. "Let's go for a walk, then. I'd like to explore."

So they had plodded the half mile up the steep lane behind Willie's house to the edge of the training area, and Dan was able at last to stand beneath the red flag and the warning signs and stare over the cattle grid into the country of his dreams.

The hills rolled away to the horizon before him and on every side. Here and there a tin shed stuck up out of the green and tawny landscape, and on one hilltop stood a tall metal structure that looked like some sort of observation post. Otherwise there was nothing to distinguish it from any other Welsh moor Dan had seen, except that this one had remained free from the growths of spruce and larch that were covering most of the hillsides Dan knew. Here, apart from the sheds and observation post, was nothing but naked mountain, reddish brown where the reeds grew, sand-colored where the dry summer grasses bent over in the breeze, a dull green where the bracken carpeted the hills in unexplained patterns. It looked like an inviting place to explore, but there was one thing missing.

"Where are the soldiers?" asked Dan.

"Probably aren't any up here," said Willie. "They aren't here all the time, you know. Can we go back now?"

Dan looked at him in surprise. "What for?" he said. "We've only just come here."

Willie didn't know why, but he was uneasy. He didn't have Dan's exploring instinct. "Mom will be wondering where we are," he said.

Dan was about to argue, but he remembered something that old Mr. Williams used to say when a young sheep dog began to get restive. "Rome wasn't built in a day," he'd remark. "We'll teach him a bit more tomorrow." Dan could look forward to a whole week of tomorrows. He could afford to be patient.

Auntie Ceinwen did not appear to have been wondering where they had gone. They played in the back garden, and when she came to call them in to supper Dan guessed she had probably never realized they had been beyond the garden gate at all.

After supper, when the entire family was watching television, the picture kept breaking into dancing parallel lines and then recovering again. After the fourth time, Marie said, "Must be the army, darn them."

Nobody else made any comment. They just sat patiently watching the flickering screen. Dan remembered what Willie had told him about the army convoys making the television go funny, and he leaped to his feet.

"Come on," he said to Willie. "Let's go and watch."

Outside, it was cool and spacious, and the smell of diesel fumes hung excitingly in the air. Dan felt the front door shake under his hand as a huge tractor trailer eased itself around the corner into the narrow lane and with a roar heaved its great weight up the steep incline. It was carrying some kind of tracked vehicle, like a small tank, on the back, with a gun sticking out from it, pointing at the faint stars.

Next came four or five trucks covered in khaki canvas and filled with soldiers, each load lit up by the lights of the vehicle following. When the soldiers saw the two boys leaning over the garden gate they all waved and hailed them. Dan and Willie waved back, silently.

Behind came armored cars, some of them towing gun carriages, then a Land Rover, the radio antenna waving high

—Dan could see a soldier inside, wearing earphones and talking into a microphone—then some more trucks full of soldiers and finally another Land Rover.

"What are they all going to do?" asked Dan.

"Night maneuvers," said Willie.

"What does that mean?"

But Willie did not know. It was just a phrase he had picked up.

"I wish we could go up there, now," said Dan. But he knew it was impossible. "We'll go there first thing tomorrow, shall we?"

"I don't mind," said Willie.

Contentment had settled back upon the rest of the family now that the interference was over. "Time you boys were in bed," said Auntie Ceinwen, peacefully, and not looking as though she intended to do anything about it.

Willie merely ignored the remark and sat down. Dan stood around, fidgeting. "I think I'll go up, then," he said after a moment. "I've got to unpack my suitcase," he added with careless pride. He had a pair of pajamas upstairs that he hadn't worn before—not new, of course, because they had belonged to Jimmy, but new to him.

Nobody responded. "Good night, then," he said hopefully.

"You better go with him, Willie," said Shirley absently, but Willie was not accustomed to going up until the end of a program.

Dan walked out of the room and up the stairs to the room where he was to sleep, feeling suddenly homesick.

The bedroom looked horrible. There was nothing particularly the matter with it, except that it was different from Dan's own bedroom. Dan's bedroom had two sorts of feeling about it, both familiar and friendly. There was the private, harborlike feeling when Dan went to bed, when it was his room and his alone, in which to dream his own dreams undisturbed. Then, if he should still be awake when Jimmy came to bed, and in the mornings, it was private in a different way, a shared privacy, when they talked and played together much more companionably than they ever did by day when the rest of the family were around.

There was nothing either private or companionable about Willie's room, in Dan's eyes. For one thing, they had to share it with Auntie Ceinwen. There were only two bedrooms in the house. The two girls shared one, and Willie slept with his mother in the other. Normally Auntie Ceinwen slept in a large, rather sagging bed in the corner, and Willie on a small sofa, but during Dan's visit Auntie Ceinwen had removed herself to the sofa and left the larger bed for Willie and Dan to share. It was not an arrangement Dan felt he would like at all, now that he stood alone and tired in the cramped space between the two beds.

Everything about the room was wrong. He did not like the pattern of the wallpaper, or the blankets on the bed. The ornaments on the mantelshelf were dull, and so were the two framed pictures, one of a cottage garden and one of a tree and a pool. There were no frayed football posters stuck lopsided on the walls, or unfinished model kits, or any of the other bits and pieces of a boy's life. This was Auntie Ceinwen's room, not Willie's.

I want to go home, I want to go home, Dan thought, taking off his shoes and socks. The cracked linoleum was cheerless beneath his bare feet. At home the floor was covered with a cut-down piece of old carpet. Dan knew every stain and worn patch like the face of a friend.

He jumped on the bed and sat there, hugging his uncomfortable suitcase, the only familiar object in the room, and realized that it was no use running downstairs to Auntie Ceinwen asking to be taken home. She had no car, and no telephone.

Strangely, that thought brought a degree of comfort. If it had simply been pride that was keeping him from giving way to homesickness, he might have run downstairs crying. But as soon as he realized that whatever he did or felt, he would still have to spend the night where he was, he began to feel a little better. Swallowing several times to relieve the tightness in his throat, he opened the suitcase and took out his pajamas. As he shook them, something fell out and rolled under the bed, so he climbed down and felt underneath to discover what it was.

It was Ferdinand, a small, bald donkey, straw-stuffed, knock-kneed, one-eared, an animal that he had used to treasure dearly, but had lately rather forgotten about, though it still lived on the window sill by his bed. When he had been packing his things, it had never occurred to him to take his donkey. What, he wondered, had induced his mother to roll Ferdinand up in his pajamas?

Suddenly, the room seemed more friendly. "Come on, Ferdinand," said Dan, "let's unpack."

He pulled a few things out of the suitcase, but it was a little difficult to do much with them while holding Ferdinand, and anyhow the happiest place for his belongings seemed to be back in the suitcase, so he bundled them all in again, and put the suitcase on the floor at the side of the bed. That way, he could reach all his things in the night.

"Let's draw the curtains," he said to Ferdinand, and it was only when he stood by the window, trying one-handedly to make the flimsy cotton curtains meet, that he realized his window looked straight out toward the hills.

"Look, Ferdinand," he said, "that's the army training area. We're going to explore it tomorrow."

As he spoke, a light streaked up out of the darkness into the sky, hung there, expanding like a flower, and then sank slowly back toward land, illuminating as it did so some of the dark contours of moorland. Then he heard the drone of a helicopter, and the put-put-put of machine-gun fire. "Oh, boy," he said, scratching his cheek on Ferdinand's haunch, "this is going to be great. I'm glad we came."

2
Operation Ferret

In the mornings during the summer season Willie's mother worked at a local hotel, and as Shirley now went to work too, it fell to Marie to look after Willie and Dan and see that they had something to eat at midday. Usually Marie passed the time by strolling down to Penbont and sitting in the park with a friend while Willie amused himself on the swings, but that was not what Dan had come for at all.

"We won't need to come downtown with you," he said politely, as soon as Mrs. Tucker and Shirley were out of the way. "Willie's going to show me around, aren't you, Willie?"

Marie looked doubtful, so Dan went on quickly. "He's seen all around my place when he's been staying with us. And anyway, I know Penbont because I've been to the market with Dan. Mom always lets us go off on our own at home, doesn't she, Willie? And it would be nicer for you, not to be bothered with us."

Marie agreed about that, anyhow. "Mind you don't get into mischief, then," she said.

"What if we get hungry?" asked Willie.

"I'll be back to get you your lunch," said Marie resignedly.

"What have we got?" said Dan. "Can't we get it for ourselves?"

The answer seemed to be a sandwich and an apple. "Mom feeds us when she gets back," said Willie.

"You don't have to come all the way back to give us that," said Dan. "We'll look after ourselves."

As soon as Marie had gone, Dan took out the sandwiches and apples and stowed them in their pockets.

"Come on," he said to Willie. "We'll take our food with us." He did not trouble to say where.

"Mom will wonder where we are when she gets back, if we're not home."

"We've got five hours," said Dan. "We can do a lot in that time."

Much had happened up on the training area since the previous evening. From far below, as they toiled up the hill, they could see the square outlines of vehicles parked along the road on the horizon. Four helicopters buzzed around above their heads, and once they had to flatten themselves against the bank as a Land Rover zipped past them unexpectedly on a narrow corner. When they came in sight of the cattle grid, they saw a large army truck parked across the entrance and beyond it groups of soldiers unloading equipment. They all carried rifles and wore camouflage netting over their helmets. Some of the men were sticking pieces of fern into the netting, and others were blacking their faces.

Nobody saw Dan and Willie arrive. The truck parked across the grid was meant to stop ordinary traffic from driving past, but it was easy for the boys to slip around its back, and they stood for quite a long time in its shadow watching all the activity before anyone noticed them.

Then a grocer's van drew up and hooted loudly to attract the attention of the lance corporal who was supposed to watch the civilian traffic that used the road. He came and opened the gate alongside the cattle grid and told the driver he could drive on

across the range since there was no firing going on. As the grocer drove off, the soldier swung the gate shut again and it was then that his eye fell upon the boys.

"Hello!" he said. "Where did you come from?"

"We walked up," said Dan. "From the cottage down there."

"Oh, aye?"

"We saw all the stuff go by last night."

"So you came to have a look."

"Yes," said Dan. "Does it matter?"

The lance corporal looked over to them, as though sizing up the situation. "I can't see why it should," he remarked. He nodded toward a little tin hut. "That's my sentry box," he said. "Just like the ones outside Buckingham Palace."

"They're not like that, are they?" said Dan disbelievingly, and the soldier laughed.

"I reckon not," he said. "But you can go and take up sentry duty in there if you like."

While Dan and Willie were taking turns at being sentries, a gloomy-looking young soldier with a blackened face sauntered over carrying his helmet and a handful of crumpled fern.

"Hey, Ted," he said, "help me fix this flippin' decoration in my helmet. I can't make it stick."

"Give it to me, Ernest," said Ted. "What have you been doing with it? Chewing the cud? Hey, young fellow-me-lad," he added to Dan, "run over and get us some decent greenery. Take my pocket knife, else you'll cut yourself on the stems."

Dan shot off and returned with an armful of fern, which Ted, the older man, wove skillfully into the netting.

"Missed my vocation, I reckon," he said. "Would have made a lovely milliner." He handed the hat back to the gloomy Ernest. "There you are, madam," he said. "Just the thing for your daughter's wedding. Five pounds, that will be."

Ernest took it, unsmiling, and crammed it on his head.

"Cheerful feller," remarked Ted to the boys.

"All very well for you," said Ernest. "I wouldn't mind your job, sitting in a cozy little box all day chatting with the locals. What about me, crawling around this mountain like a bloomin' Red Indian? Look at it," he added, staring around. "Miles and miles of it, in every direction. And I've got to make my way from Point A to Point B not only without getting lost, but without being spotted by the enemy, either."

"The enemy?" said Dan, eagerly.

"Company B," said Ernest. "Company A, we are."

"Go on," said Dan.

"You tell 'em," said Ernest to Ted. "I've got to collect my rations." He moved off to a truck, newly arrived, where an orderly was doling out sandwiches and cake.

"It's what our commanding officer calls a field-course exercise," said Ted. "They've got to locate the enemy advance post somewhere in these hills. 'Operation Ferret' this exercise is."

"How do they know where to go?" asked Dan. "And what are they looking for, anyhow?"

"A truck like this one, most probably, or a Land Rover, tucked away somewhere, with a white pennant, so they know they've found the right place—the sergeant in charge of each section will have a map reference he'll be telling the men about. Then when they get there they report to the officer in charge —unless they get captured on the way, of course."

"By the enemy?"

"Yeah. They're lurking around, and if they see one of our fellows they challenge him, and then he has to act as though he's captured and go to the enemy's base."

"Like a prisoner-of-war camp?"

"Sort of, I suppose. It's just a building by the small-arms range, where they do the firing at other times."

"I hope we win," said Dan.

"Joined Company A, have you?" Dan nodded.

Ernest came back. "It's starting to rain," he said. "If that isn't the limit."

"You two kids are going to get wet," said Ted. "How long will it take you to run home?"

"We don't mind getting wet, do we, Willie?"

Willie did not seem too sure.

"Tell you what," said Ted. "It's coming down heavy now, but it don't look as though it will last long. You slip into the back of that truck until the worst is over, then you can run along home."

"Won't anyone mind?" asked Dan, already scrambling up.

"They won't have to know, will they?" said Ted, giving Willie a leg up. "Anyway, I don't suppose anyone will notice."

One of the trucks nearby burst into life as the driver started the engine, and Dan peered out nervously.

"It won't go off with us inside, will it?" he asked.

"Don't you worry," said Ted. "Those trucks are transporting the various sections to their starting points, but this one

isn't. It's just being used to block the road. Hang on, there's another civilian van coming up."

Ted went off to let a butcher's van through the gate, and then retired into his sentry box out of the driving rain.

It was fun in the truck. There was nothing much inside it except a heavy wooden box with a red cross on the outside, and a bundle of very thick rope and some tarpaulins, but it smelled excitingly of grease and wet canvas and soldiers' boots. The back end overlooked the sentry box, where Ted was struggling into a waterproof cape, so Dan went forward and discovered he could pull the canvas cover of the truck to make a crack through which they could watch Company A getting into their sections ready to be driven off to their various starting places. An officer walked over past them and Dan slipped to the back of the truck. He could see the officer was talking to Ted. He seemed to be

sending him on an errand because Ted walked off up the road.
The rain was easing off.

"We ought to go," said Dan, "but we'd better stay in here
until that officer moves away. We don't want to get Ted into
trouble for letting us get in here."

All the other vehicles were now lined up ready to start, except
for one other truck standing on the grass near their own. A
soldier jumped down from the cab of that one and walked across
and spoke to the officer by Ted's sentry box.

"Won't start?" they heard the officer say. "Oh, well, take the
other one, then, and ask them to send a mechanic down from
headquarters."

The soldier saluted and walked straight back toward them, so
that Dan and Willie hastily crouched down behind the tarpaulins. The next instant, the door of their cab slammed, the
truck roared, shook, and pulled smartly away in a semicircle
over the rough ground, regained the road and bowled away up
the road.

3
Stranded

In the first startled moment, Dan leaped to his feet, but was instantly flung back onto the floor as they jolted over the rough ground. He looked across at Willie, at first in consternation, but the sight of Willie's horror-struck expression appealed to his sense of humor and he began to giggle weakly and then went into peals of laughter.

"I don't see what's so funny," said Willie, in a trembly voice. "Can't you stop it, *please?*"

Dan tried once more to get to his feet, but the swaying truck made it impossible for him to keep his balance, and he was thrown back onto the tarpaulin. He edged himself along on his hands and knees and peered cautiously over the tailgate. They were just topping the first rise, and for a moment he had a view of a cluster of soldiers and the line of trucks by the cattle grid, fast receding into the distance; then they disappeared from view behind the brow of the hill. Empty moorland rolled out behind them like a carpet. The truck showed no signs of stopping.

"What are we going to do?" asked Willie, scrambling up beside him. Dan edged himself into a sitting position on the end of the roll of tarpaulin.

"There's not much we can do," he said. He looked at the woebegone Willie. "There's nothing really to worry about," he said kindly. "It's not our fault we're here, so they really can't be cross with us when they find out."

"Yes, but how are we going to get home?" asked Willie. "We're going on forever."

Indeed, the road slipped away behind them at an alarming rate, but distances always seem longer when you don't know where you are going. In fact, they had not traveled more than three miles when the truck suddenly swung off to the right onto a metal army track. Soon after, it slowed down and pulled up. The engine died away, and in the silence they heard the driver jump down from the cab, slamming the door behind him. Unable to decide whether to leap out or to hide, the two boys sat quite still, but nobody appeared at the back of the truck. Dan crept across and peered out through the crack between the cab and the canvas cover, first on one side of the truck, and then the other.

On the right there was a brick building, with a Land Rover parked nearby. Beyond and around it were various artificial mounds—bunkers, Dan thought. To the left was open ground, sloping upward, and all over this grassy slope targets were scattered around, including some cut-out shapes of human figures. Farther up, a couple of dummy tanks stood on a short stretch of railway track. They were attached to wires, so that they could be pulled to and fro to provide a moving target. The army road appeared to come to a dead end and served only to link the building with the main road.

"I know where we are," said Dan. "This is the small-arms range Ted was talking about."

"Will we get shot?" asked Willie nervously.

"Of course not," said Dan. "They wouldn't shoot one of their own trucks—at least I hope not. Ssh!"

Two soldiers had come out of the building carrying a heavy-looking tool bag, and flung it with a clatter into the back of the Land Rover. One of the men Dan recognized as the driver of their own truck, and the other was presumably the mechanic sent for to repair the broken-down truck, because he climbed into the Land Rover and bumped away up the road the way they

had come. Their own driver glanced for a moment toward their truck, as though wondering whether to get anything out of it, and then turned away and went back into the building. Both boys breathed again.

"If this is the firing range, then I bet that's the building where they keep all the men who get captured. Remember?"

"Oh, no," said Willie. "Will they keep us prisoners there, too, if they capture us?" It was easy to feel that this was a real war, with real enemies and real battles.

"No," said Dan. "Of course not. At least . . . well, I wouldn't think so. Anyway," he added, not feeling too sure himself about it, "we'll make sure we're not caught. Let's make a break for it now."

He slid one leg over the tailgate and perched there a moment, looking left and right. Then he slipped down to the ground and waited, flattened against the truck, for Willie to join him. He put out a hasty arm to stop Willie from tumbling forward onto his nose, then darted across the gap between the truck and the building, and flattened himself once more against the brick wall. Willie copied him faithfully, although he was not the right shape for flattening, really.

"Where do we go now?" said Willie.

"You stay here till I get to the next hideout, then when I wave, run over and join me," said Dan. He started off, bent double, for the ditch alongside the road they had driven along. Willie felt very visible stuck up against the wall all by himself. When Dan, peering ahead over the road, flung out his arm behind him to beckon, he knocked Willie on the nose.

"Ow!" said Willie.

"You weren't to come *with* me," said Dan. "You were to wait till I got here, I said."

"Yes," said Willie.

Bending low again, Dan ran a little way along the side of the bank, then darted across to a convenient bunker. This time Willie waited for as long as he dared, but when he saw Dan head away from the bank, he could see the bunker he was aiming for, and cut straight across. They arrived at the bunker at the same moment.

"Beat you," said Willie, hoping he had scored a point, but from Dan's look he could see he had done the wrong thing again.

"Now stay here," said Dan, "until I signal. Right?"

"Yes," said Willie. Dan prepared to make another dash, but Willie caught him and pulled him back.

"Why?" said Willie. "Why can't I come with you?"

Dan did a quick think. "It's like on TV. It's so if one man goes ahead and gets shot, then the other man knows it's not safe to come. Or if the second man gets shot, the first still has a chance to get through." He ran on again, and Willie was so busy turning this explanation over in his mind that he forgot to look where Dan had gone. As soon as he realized this, he rushed out, gazing wildly in every direction. Ahead of him the level ground stretched away into the distance, covered with brownish grass and dotted with the white blobs of cotton grass. A large rock stuck up, with a gorse bush growing aslant from the base. To the left was the brick building and the truck; to the right, the metal track led up to the road.

Willie guessed Dan must be behind the rock, and as he dashed toward it Dan's last words echoed in his mind. He was in full view of the building. What if the soldier had come out and even now stood with a machine-gun leveled at him, finger on the trigger? He dared not look in that direction, but stumbled forward, expecting at any moment to hear the stutter of machine-gun fire, and to fall crumpling down in the bog.

For bog it was. As each foot squelched farther into the mire than the last, Willie was brought to a despairing halt.

"Dan!" he cried aloud, for all to hear. "Where are you?"

"Here!" cried Dan, rising up out of a clump of bracken on the slope below the road and sinking hurriedly back down again. But Willie, panic-stricken, turned too blindly to spot him before he disappeared again.

"Where?" he bawled.

Dan, worried about the noise Willie was making, bolted from his hiding place, seized Willie, and ran back with him to the bracken. There, in a fierce whisper, he explained about moving behind enemy lines, while Willie gulped and sobbed and listened to not a word.

"Please," he said when Dan had finished, "can we go together next time?"

Dan surveyed his dirt-and-tear-streaked assistant with a twinge of compassion. "Yes," he said, "we'll do that. Be more fun. After all, there isn't *really* any danger of getting shot."

Willie made no reply.

Dan reared up in the bracken like a rabbit and looked cautiously around. He could see that the boggy area where Willie had been heading stretched away into the distance, perfectly level. It ran more or less back in the direction they had come in the truck, but sloping diagonally away from it, so that if they

tried to make their way home that way they would end up on the
wrong side of a small hill. In any case, there was no cover.
Nothing interesting could be hidden there, nor could they hide
there themselves. He turned around the other way, and looked
over the army track, to where the main road looped away along
the side of the valley. A glint of light by a bridge caught his eye.
Was that smudgy lump of greenery a bush, or a clump of fern, or
was it a camouflaged soldier, keeping a lookout through binoculars? There was another glint, and then the clump seemed to
reform itself, so that it had two heads.

"That's the enemy," said Dan.

"How do you know?"

"Must be. Let's go and see what they're up to."

"No!" said Willie.

"It's not far. It'll only take a few minutes."

"I don't want to," said Willie, unexpectedly stubborn.
"We've got miles to get home, as it is."

Just then a ttruck lumbered into view out of a fold in the hills where a stream ran down, and stopped on the bridge by the two lookout men, who were now clearly visible. A second truck started to pull up behind it, but seemed to get stuck in the mud. It gave out a lot of roaring and grinding noises, but did not move. Both drivers and the two lookout men went and stood around it, obviously discussing what to do next.

"Come on," said Dan. "Let's go and see what's happening down there."

"We can't," said Willie. "Not if they're watching this way."

"They're not," said Dan. He wormed his way along until he came to the edge of the bracken. From here they could get a better view and could hear the men talking. One of the drivers was fixing a towrope between the two trucks. The lookout men were getting restive, and kept glancing up around the surrounding hills.

"For Pete's sake," they heard one of them say, "get that truck out and look sharp about it. If the attackers come into view now, the game will be up before it's even started."

"Okay, ready to go," said the driver, climbing up into his cab.

The second driver had been at the back of the stranded truck, but now he, too, got in and started up the engine.

"Hold those sacks down under the back wheels," he called to the lookout men, who ran around to the sunken back end of the truck, where they were hidden from view.

"Quick!" said Dan. "Now!" He ran forward, looking wildly for cover, but finding none. The only possible place to hide was in the actual streambed just below the bridge, which meant running across an open space for about two hundred yards, almost directly toward the soldiers. However, they were busy with the trucks, and the engines made so much noise that there was no danger of their hearing the boys. Dan grabbed Willie by the hand and dragged him helter-skelter over rocks and anthills and tussocks of coarse grass until they tumbled, puffing, into the shelter of the streambed. Just then, the second truck lurched up onto the road, and the two lookouts came back onto the bridge.

"Now clear off, and stop hanging around," they heard the leader say. "Once the attackers get a sight of those big trucks they'll guess where the advance post is. Go on—beat it."

The second lookout man was struggling to release the tow-rope, and the speaker, with an impatient exclamation, went over to help him. Dan at once started to scramble up the shallow streambed, tugging Willie after him, slipping and splashing among the rocks until they were under the bridge itself.

"Why here?" gasped Willie.

"Ssh!" said Dan, though there was little danger of their voices carrying above the clatter of the brook and the rumble of the retreating trucks.

It was an excellent hiding place, for there was some dry

gravel to stand on and even a low concrete ledge to sit on, but it was also a trap. In the quiet after the trucks had moved off they could hear the two men moving around and talking above them. It was plain they were standing on each side of the bridge, keeping watch, one over the low-lying target area, the other over the uplands above the road.

"What do we do now?" asked Willie, when he had his breath back. He was past being frightened, and had resigned himself to following Dan around on this mad adventure.

"We'll rest a bit," said Dan, "and see what happens."

Willie, sitting doubled up under the bridge, became conscious of a bulge in his jeans pocket. "Can we eat our sandwiches?" he asked.

4
Under the Nose of the Enemy

Dan thought that was the best idea Willie had ever come up with. Under the bridge they sat and munched companionably, while above their heads the enemy scanned the landscape. Crawling on your stomach over a mountain is not very good for crumbly objects stuffed into front trouser pockets, but the taste was all right by the time they had sorted out the bits of fluff and grit that seemed to have gotten mixed up with the bread. Afterward they ate the battered apples—crawling would be much easier without them, as Dan pointed out.

When they had finished, they continued to sit, getting rather cold under the dank bridge and wondering how to get away.

"Now we know that the advance post is somewhere around here, we really ought to find Ernest and tell him," said Dan.

"How?" said Willie.

"You think of something for a change," said Dan, a little crossly.

Willie thought. After a while he spoke.

"Either we stay here till they go away . . ."

"Which might mean all day."

". . . or we give ourselves up."

"We won't do that," said Dan. "Not yet."

Suddenly the man above them spoke. He was the one with the binoculars, and seemed to be the leader.

"I'll just take a look up the road, and see if I can spot any signs of life."

"Watch they don't spot you first."

"What d'you take me for?"

"Go ahead then."

"You cover my side of the bridge, then, while I'm gone."

"Okay."

The boys could hear the soldier's boots tramping away up the road.

"We've got a chance now," whispered Dan. "The other man can't watch both sides at once."

"How will we know which side he *is* watching?"

"Ssh!" said Dan. He made his way to the very edge of the bridge and looked cautiously up, straight at the soles of a pair of hobnailed boots dangling not a yard above his head. The enemy must have been sitting on the wall. As he looked the boots began to move, and Dan ducked quickly back. There was a scraping sound on the roadway.

"Perhaps he's gone across now," said Dan. "I'll take another look."

The boots had vanished, and Dan stepped cautiously up onto the grassy bank and peered over the wall. He was just in time to see the soldier pick up the binoculars from the other side and turn to come straight back.

Dan had no time to do anything except drop to the ground and lie there, motionless, face down, knowing that he must be in full view if the soldier should happen to look down.

He lay there for several seconds, like an ostrich, and nothing happened. Then, very cautiously, he turned his head sideways. First Willie's face under the arch came into view, looking scared. He tilted his head another inch, and got the soldier into his line of vision. The only reason he had not been seen was because the soldier had the binoculars and was studying the hillside above them. Perhaps some movement up there had attracted his attention. As soon as he took his binoculars down, Dan thought he could hardly help but see him lying on the bank below him.

He looked quickly to right and left. He was too far from the bridge to make it back there, especially as he would not be able to slide quickly down into the stream without making a noise. Beside him, a flat space had been scooped out of the hillside to make a turning place for vehicles. It was mostly dry and stony, but near Dan there were deep wheel marks in the mud where the truck must have gone too close to the stream. Then he saw something else—the sacks that the driver had put under the back wheels to stop the skidding.

Dan glanced back at the soldier, who was still looking through the binoculars, but not so intently. He was sweeping the hillside with the binoculars in a general sort of way, and Dan felt sure he was just about to bring them down. Quickly, Dan rolled over into the wheel rut and pulled the sack over him, making sure he had a crack through which he could keep watch on the soldier.

He felt certain his legs were sticking out at the other end of the sack, and was wondering whether he dare move them when the soldier put down the binoculars. For what seemed a terribly long time, nobody moved—the soldier on the bridge, Willie under the bridge, Dan lying in the mud under the wet sack.

Then there was a distraction. "Hey!" came the voice of the man up the road. "Bring those glasses up here a minute. I think I can see some of them moving right over beyond the target area."

"Whereabouts?"

"You can't see from down there. Come up here a minute."

The boys could hear the heavy boots clumping away up the road. Like a flash, Dan was out from under the sack, grabbed Willie, who was waiting under the arch, bolted upstream, around the corner out of sight of the bridge, and tumbled into the thick bracken which grew there right down to the stream itself.

"We've made it," exclaimed Dan, in a joyful whisper, as soon as he could get his breath back. "We'll follow along by the stream for a bit," he went on. "It's best to get farther away from the road before we start making our way home." Privately, he was still hoping to find the enemy's advance post, but he thought it wiser not to mention this to Willie at present.

They wove their way between the bracken stalks, bending low to avoid being seen. All the time, Dan was wondering about the advance post, but because he was keeping his head down so carefully he did not see it until it was quite literally on top of him. Suddenly everything darkened, and Dan looked up, thinking he must have come under the shadow of a big rock or tree, and found himself almost under the hood of a Land Rover.

He backed away till he was alongside Willie, and motioned him to keep very still. Then he pointed to the Land Rover.

"Is anyone in it?" whispered Willie.

"Don't know. We'll have to find out." Dan raised his head and looked around. No one was in sight, so he rose a little higher. Now he could see the Land Rover clearly, and the white flag flying from the hood. Then a sudden noise made them both drop flat on their faces.

It was the sound of thudding footsteps and heavy breathing. The next instant a pair of large boots passed so close to them in the bracken that Willie nearly had his hand trampled on. Luckily the runner was more interested in speed than in looking around, and as he rounded the back of the vehicle they heard the voice of another man.

"Ah, so one of you has made it. That was pretty quick." From his voice, the speaker sounded like a young officer, and he must have been standing all the time on the farther side of the Land Rover.

"Member of attacking party, come to report," said the other man, rather out of breath.

"You've not taken long," commented the officer. "I wasn't expecting any of you just yet. Come over here so that I can make a note of your section and so forth."

The two men suddenly appeared in view on the far side of the
Land Rover's hood, upon which the officer rested his papers in
order to note down the soldier's arrival.

Greatly daring, Dan crawled closer in under the shadow of
the vehicle itself, and then scuttled around to the back, with
Willie at his heels. Luckily the Land Rover had been driven into
a clump of good thick fern, so they had plenty of cover.

Dan wanted to get as far away from the soldiers as he could,
but he resisted the temptation to make a bolt for it because the
waving fronds would give them away. Instead, he crawled
along with caution, steering between the stems rather than
knocking them down, until a sharp bend in the gully took them
out of view.

When he looked back and saw that the men were out of sight,
he heaved a sigh of relief. Now they could get along faster, but
he still made Willie keep to his hands and knees, fearing that
there might be other attackers making their way to the Land

Rover. He was getting worried, because they were still miles from home, and at this rate they would never get back. He was beginning to feel pretty tired, too.

Just then, he bumped into a wire fence, which brought him to so sudden a halt that Willie, following close behind him, knelt on his ankle.

"Ow!" said Dan.

"Sorry. What are you stopping for?"

"I've come up against a fence. Come and see."

Willie edged up beside him. The fence was made of strong wire mesh, stretched straight and taut between stout concrete posts, and looked higher than an ordinary farm fence.

"Oh, yeah," said Willie, without a trace of surprise in his voice, "that will be the boundary fence."

"The *boundary* fence?"

"Yeah, that's right."

"Do you *know* where we are?"

"There's a farm up there, Prosser's, where Mom goes at Christmastime to feather turkeys. I've been up with her a couple of times. The lane runs all along the boundary fence. I remember seeing it."

"Why ever didn't you say before?"

"I didn't know till I got here, did I? Anyway, you never asked."

Dan sighed. "If we climb over the fence and walk down the lane, how far is it back to your place?"

"About two miles."

"But that's easy. Much shorter than going back across the mountains, and no one can catch us."

Dan pulled at the taut bottom wire, to see if there was any chance of crawling under it, but there was not. "We will have to climb over, and just hope nobody sees us," he said.

"People aren't allowed to climb the boundary fence," said Willie solemnly. "They've got notices all along the other side, saying 'Ministry of Defense Keep Out.' "

"Well, so long as they haven't got notices on this side saying 'Keep In,' it's okay," said Dan with a grin, but Willie's expression remained blank.

Climbing the fence took some time. It was high and awkward, with a barbed-wire strand running along the top, too tightly stretched to allow them to squeeze beneath it, so they had to climb carefully over, wobbling dangerously and very much exposed to view.

Eventually Dan jumped clear, but Willie cried out as the barbed-wire caught his jeans between the legs, and he was unable to get free.

"Ssh!" said Dan, climbing back up and trying to disentangle him, but almost at the same moment a man's voice shouted, "Hey! What are you kids doing?"

Willie flung himself to the ground on the lane side, tearing his jeans in the process, but Dan stayed on the fence looking over, eagerly scanning the hillside. "Just looking," he said to the soldier who had caught them.

"Why are you there?"

"Just going down the lane."

"Can't you see the 'Keep Out' notices?"

"I am keeping out," said Dan.

"Don't tell me you weren't trying to climb in over that fence when I caught you."

"We weren't," said Dan, with absolute truth. "Were we, Willie?"

"No," said Willie nervously.

The soldier began to walk over to them. Dan had a flash of inspiration. "We were watching all those soldiers climbing over the mountain," he said, nodding vaguely toward the hill behind the soldier.

It was an unfortunate remark. Though Dan did not know it, there was indeed a party of Company A making their way along the hillside, very slowly because the cover there was sparse, and they were trying to avoid detection by the defender at the fence.

Now, seeing him occupied by a couple of children, they had decided at that moment to make a dash for it, and even as Dan spoke they rose up out of the ground before his startled eyes and raced across the moorland.

Fortunately, the soldier did not believe Dan right away.

"What soldiers?" he said, but then, seeing Dan's expression, he turned to follow the direction of his eyes. By that time, five out of the six attackers had slid into the fern, but he saw the sixth.

"Halt, or I fire!" he shouted, and to the horror of Dan and Willie he did indeed bring up his rifle and point it directly at the bracken where the man had disappeared.

"Don't shoot!" cried Dan, in simple panic, but at the same moment the man on the hillside scrambled meekly to his feet and came toward them, his hands above his head.

"Thanks for the tip," said the defender, to Dan's shame, and added with a laugh, "It's all right, it's not loaded, don't you worry," and strode off to make sure of his captive.

"Come on," said Willie. It was good advice, because Dan had been too absorbed in the capture to think about their own escape. Quickly they ran off together down the lane.

5
Friend or Foe

Half an hour later, they dropped off the open moorland into a small wooded valley which, following the course of a brook, ran up into the heart of the training area. The fence had to plunge down a steep slope to the water and climb up again on the far side among a jumble of rocks and trees before it could regain its course along the level upland. Here the lane Dan and Willie were following parted company from the fence, and followed the brook down the valley.

Sitting on a rock by the stream, with his back to them, just inside the boundary fence, was a soldier, chin in hand, staring moodily at the burbling water.

Dan saw him first, and motioned to Willie to pass by quietly, so as not to arouse his attention—he had had enough of soldiers for one day.

But after they had passed, Willie whispered, "That was Ernest."

"No!" said Dan. "Was it?"

"Yeah. I'm sure."

"We only saw his back." Dan looked back. It could be—but then one soldier in battle dress, with a blackened face, was very much like another.

"I'm certain," said Willie. "Look at his hat."

Dan looked, and saw at once what Willie meant. That fanci-

ful array of fern, so elegantly arranged, could only be Ted's handiwork.

Dan retraced his steps and spoke through the fence. "Hello," he said.

Willie had not made a mistake. It was Ernest's gloomy face that looked around at them.

"Boy!" he said. "You kids really get around."

"We're just on our way home," said Willie. There was something about Ernest that touched a responsive chord in Willie, and he became quite forthcoming.

"I wish I was," said Ernest. "Haven't got anything to eat on you, I suppose? My lunch was nothing but crumbs by the time I got around to it."

The boys shook their heads. They knew just how he felt.

"What are you doing here?" asked Dan. "What are you waiting for?"

"Christmas," said Ernest. He picked up a stone and chucked it into the brook.

"You'll be even hungrier by then," said Willie, unexpectedly producing a joke. Dan gave a surprised grin, but Ernest was pursuing his own line of thought.

"Gone and lost myself, that's what I've done," he said. "Told you I would, didn't I?"

"How, lost?" said Dan. "Where are you supposed to be?"

"At the enemy advance post, I guess. But if I could just meet up with one of them defenders and get myself captured, that would suit me all right. I reckon I'm the only human being on this mountain, bar you two jokers."

"Oh, no," said Willie. "We've seen lots more, and the advance post, and the sentries, and everything." Dan gave him a warning look, but for Willie, Ernest wasn't like the other soldiers; he was an old friend.

"Where?" said Ernest, unimpressed.

"It's . . . you explain, Dan. It's by a stream."

"No," said Ernest. "That's where you're wrong. Heard them say that, did you? Yeah, that's what my sergeant said. 'It'll be by the stream,' he said, 'up some little valley.' And he told us all to fan out and creep over the hill till we came to the stream, and then follow it up and it would bring us to the enemy headquarters. So that's what I done, and it's brought me here, to the boundary fence, and not a vehicle nor a soldier in sight. So much for his bright little idea."

"This is the wrong stream," said Dan. "And anyway, you've been following it down, not up."

"Up or down, it don't make sense to me," said Ernest. "Sticking a fellow down in a place like this, no street signs, no pubs—how can I tell which way I'm going?"

"I know," said Willie, with modest pride. "See, supposing

this is the boundary fence, where we are now—" he laid a twig along the ground on his side of the fence, and scooped up a handful of stones from the bottom of the brook to mark out each place as he mentioned it—"the cattle grid, where you started from, is, say, here, and this stream must run down something like this. Then the other stream runs along like this, and there's this big hill here, and Prosser's farm would be about here—no, here—and then the bridge would be about here, and the enemy . . ."

"Hang on," said Dan, surprised at Willie's accurate sense of direction. "You mustn't tell him where the advance post is till he promises."

"Oh, yes," said Willie. "You've got to promise."

"Promise what?" said Ernest, staring at Willie's map with deep attention.

"Not to tell anyone where we've been."

"The strain will kill me," said Ernest. "What would I want to do that for? I couldn't care less where you've been."

"Promise? You've got to promise," said Dan.

"Yeah, yeah, I promise. Does that mean then, that if I go on up this fence, here, I come to another stream?"

Patiently, Willie explained his map, over and over again, pointing out the hill and fence and direction of stream. Ernest drank it all in like a man to whom a mystery is suddenly made plain.

"Yeah," he said. "I see it now. It kind of makes sense, this way. I never could understand what the sergeant was on about with his maps and compasses, but like this, it makes sense." He looked up from the twigs and stones to the surrounding landscape. "Now, where's this advance post?"

"Can I tell him, Dan?"

"Yeah, go ahead."

"It's here," said Willie, laying a convenient rabbit dropping on the line of leaves. "That's right, isn't it, Dan?"

"Bit farther down, I'd say," said Dan.

"How d'you know?" asked Ernest.

"You tell him, Dan."

Dan launched eagerly into an account of their activities, but Ernest was not really interested. All he wanted was to be sure that the boys really did know what they were talking about. He kept on interrupting Dan's tale by asking Willie to explain about his map again.

"Right," he said at last. "I'd better get moving." He assembled his pack, his rifle, and his decorated hat, and looked about him. "I go along this fence, okay?"

"Right," said Dan.

"How do I know when to turn off? I don't want that soldier by the fence to get me."

Dan described the route they had taken, while Willie pointed it out on his map. Ernest kept on asking Willie to repeat things for him. "That kid," he complained, nodding at Dan, "talks too fast."

At last he was satisfied, and turned to go.

"Thanks, kids," he said, and suddenly grinned. "I can't wait to see my sergeant's face if I make it. He was dead sure I'd be the first of his section to get captured." He turned and plunged off up the bank. The boys watched him out of sight. Then they ran all the way home.

6
In a Tight Spot

They arrived back at exactly the same moment as Willie's mother, who was climbing out of a car by the front gate.

"Alf," said Willie. "He works at the hotel. He generally brings Mom home."

Dan ran around the house and opened the gate. "Hello, Auntie Ceinwen," he said.

The car pulled off up the road, and the boys accompanied Mrs. Tucker around to the back door, which was opened by Marie, looking fretful. When she saw Dan and Willie with her mother, her expression changed.

"Where've you been?" she said.

"Playing," said Dan.

"Met me in the garden," said Auntie Ceinwen. "Been good boys, have they?"

Marie opened her mouth to say something, then thought better of it.

"Well, have they?"

Marie turned to go into the kitchen. "I haven't seen much of them all day," she muttered vaguely.

"There's good boys," said Auntie Ceinwen approvingly. "I expect you'll be wanting your tea."

Next morning, Dan was expecting a battle with Marie after her mother and sister had gone off to work, but Marie had been thinking things over and decided it was much less trouble to let Dan have his own way. All she said was, "I don't care what you do, so long as you keep out of mischief and get home before Mom does."

"What about lunch?" said Willie.

"There's bread and cheese and tomatoes, and Mom's made a chocolate cake you can have," said Marie. "If you think you can manage, I'll probably stay downtown and get some chips."

"Great," said Dan, as soon as she had gone. "Let's make sandwiches." There was a sliced loaf of bread, which made things easier, and they soon had a good filling meal ready to take with them.

Willie felt rather nervous as they trudged up the hill once more, but Dan reassured him. "We'll just see how they're getting on," he said. "We won't get into any trucks."

In fact, the day passed harmlessly enough to satisfy even Willie. They found a lot of soldiers, including Ted, but not Ernest, setting up a sort of camp near the cattle grid, and they spent a happy morning wandering around inspecting the various tents and vehicles, which were all being camouflaged. When the soldiers broke off for a meal, Dan and Willie got out their sandwiches and sat down with them.

Nobody seemed to mind having them around until the young officer in charge spotted an official-looking Land Rover approaching.

"That's the colonel," he said. "You'd best beat it."

They ran off home then, but Dan had seen a refuse dump near the encampment where the soldiers had been throwing empty cans. There seemed to be quite a lot of discarded army equipment among the rubbish, and next day Dan told Willie he wanted to go and explore it.

The place was deserted this time. All that was left of the camp were some freshly made ruts in the turf and square flattened patches where the big tents had stood, so they made their way to the refuse dump.

It proved to be an exciting place, and they spent the morning looking among the empty beer and Coke cans for used bullets and clips, which could be slotted together to make belts. They also found an old canvas bag for each of them to keep treasures in, and Willie discovered two army boots, both left feet. That did not matter, because they were much too big for him, and he clumped around with them on over his own shoes. Then Dan found a helmet, and that delayed them, because Willie wanted one too, and it took a long time to find another. It was very rusted and dented, not nearly so good as Dan's, but then, as Dan said, Willie had the boots as well.

By the time they had all they wanted, their packs were very full, so they decided to heave them over the boundary fence at the nearest point, rather than carry them all the way around by the cattle grid.

Willie insisted they should walk around themselves, however, because his mother had scolded him about his torn jeans last time. They both wore their helmets, even though the brims came down to their noses, making it difficult for them to see where they were going.

They had plenty of time to spare, so they stopped and played on the cattle grid, trying to walk from one side to the other along one of the shining rails without slipping through or putting a foot on the rails on either side. There was a space between each about four inches wide and a gap of about a foot between the rails and the bottom of the pit. Dan put one foot through each side of a rail and walked along like that to prove to Willie that falling through really was not dangerous and he could afford to be more daring.

However, he had overlooked the fact that Willie's legs were a good deal fatter than his own. When Willie did go faster, and inevitably slipped in with one foot, he found himself jammed tight.

Ten minutes later, the army colonel, driving himself home in the Land Rover with the flag, had to brake to a sudden halt to avoid running into Willie, tearful and apparently legless, sitting in the middle of the road wearing an army helmet, while Dan stood over him, trying to pull him out.

The colonel got out and walked over to them.

"How did this happen?" he asked. Dan explained while Willie sobbed despairingly.

"I see," said the colonel. "Well, we'll soon have you out, don't worry." He bent over Willie, and as he could not see much of him under the helmet, he removed it and hung it on the gatepost.

"Warning triangles," he said suddenly. Dan stared at him blankly. "This is a dangerous corner, and we ought to warn on-coming vehicles." Willie broke into fresh howls at the thought of convoys of tanks bearing down on him.

"Don't worry, old chap," said the colonel. He turned to Dan. "There should be at least one red warning sign in the back of the Land Rover. Get it and set it up. . . ." He looked both ways, trying to decide which approach was the more dangerous. "We ought to find another sign that would be suitable—there are quite a few there."

Dan ran off and found the sign, and set it out on the road just around the corner above the cattle grid. Then he went back to see what else he could find. There were no more warning signs, but there were several army signs, including one saying "Di-version," which he supposed would do. Then, as he started to pull it out, he saw one saying "Danger—Unexploded Bomb." That was much better.

"What have you got there?" asked the colonel as he passed. Dan showed him the sign and he nodded. "That'll do," he said.

"Where?" gulped Willie. "Where's the bomb?"

"Here," said the colonel. "You're the bomb. You'll have to take your trousers off."

Willie stared in panic-stricken silence for a moment, and then howled more despairingly than ever.

The colonel turned to Dan, who had come back. "You seem

to be a sensible sort of boy. Tell him he's got to take his pants off. That's what's making him stick."

Dan bent down over Willie and shouted above the roars. "He says you're to take your pants off."

Willie shook his head miserably.

"You've got to. It's . . . it's against the Queen's regulations to disobey," said Dan. Willie stared up at the colonel standing over him, resplendent in his army uniform, and fumbled with the zipper.

"I can't!" he sobbed.

Dan did it for him, and then put his hands between the bars and grasped the bottoms of Willie's trousers, while the colonel hauled from above, and up came Willie like a carrot out of the ground.

The colonel dumped him on the ground and unconcernedly passed him his jeans, rescued by Dan. Willie grabbed them and bolted for the sentry box.

Tactfully turning his back, the colonel gave his attention to Dan. "Where did you get those helmets?" he asked.

"We found them."

"Where?"

"On the dump. Does it matter?"

"There aren't any unexploded bombs on the dump, if that's what you mean. So long as you stick to helmets it's all right." Dan thought of the rest of their loot farther along the fence, and said nothing. "But it's not safe to have boys like you wandering all over the mountain, picking up interesting bits of metal. One of those could be an unexploded shell."

"Yes, sir. We weren't doing that, sir."

"I'm glad to hear it. One of my soldiers did report a couple of boys trying to climb the fence over by the small-arms range during an exercise a couple of days ago."

"Did he, sir?"

"Yes, he did. And I'm not sure you're not the boys I saw hanging around here when I drove up yesterday."

"We weren't doing anything wrong, sir."

Willie had returned, sniffing and pink, but otherwise none the worse. The colonel turned to him. "Feeling better?" he asked briskly.

"Yes, sir, thank you, sir. Can we go now?"

"That's just what you'd better do, quick sharp. And if you'll take my advice you'll keep away from the ranges from now on. You should have seen enough to satisfy your curiosity."

Willie bolted off down the road. The colonel picked his helmet off the gatepost and called after him, "Don't forget your hat." Willie paused in midflight to look back, like a wild bird weighing up the risk of taking crumbs from an outstretched hand, and then fled on.

Dan said politely, "Shall I take it for him, sir? He's shy."

"H'm" said the colonel. "Maybe that's better than being so sharp you cut yourself."

Dan took the hat without another word, and bolted after Willie as fast as he could go.

7
The Map

Next day, it was raining, and Marie stayed at home. So did Dan and Willie—Willie, at least, never wanted to set foot on the training area again.

"We've got to go to town this evening anyway," said Marie. "We've got singing practice."

"Singing practice?" asked Dan. Somehow he had never thought of the Tuckers as doing anything except eat and watch television.

"We've got to practice our songs for the eisteddfod, our singing competition, tomorrow."

"You sing in those things?" asked Dan.

Marie said, "Me and Shirl, we're singing in a duet, and then Shirl and Mom are both in the adult choir."

"And I'm singing a solo in the eleven and under class," said Willie.

"You're not!" said Dan, still more surprised.

"The judge last year said Willie had a pure little voice," said Marie, seriously.

I bet *I* could have a pure little voice if I tried, thought Dan, but who'd want to stand on a platform and sing all by himself? Aloud, he said, "Do you *like* singing?"

"I don't mind," said Willie.

"But don't you get terribly nervous?"

"I do," said Marie, happily. "I have to keep on going to the toilet, and there's always a line, and you never know when your turn's going to come, and I'm always afraid I'll miss it."

"I don't mind," said Willie again.

Dan stared at him. "Aren't there lots of people watching?"

"Oh, yes," said Marie, proudly. "Our eisteddfod is one of the most popular around here."

"Can I come?" asked Dan.

"Oh, of course, We'll all be going. It probably won't finish until two or three in the morning. It didn't last year—remember, Willie? Oh, but Willie was asleep all through the last part."

Dan thought it would be a lot of fun. "I've never stayed up as late as that," he said.

When Shirley, Marie, and Willie went off that evening, their music under their arms, Mrs. Tucker said she'd wait till Marie and Willie came home before she went down to join Shirley for the choir practice, so that Dan would not be left at home on his own.

"But then you'll miss part of it," said Dan, who had ideas of his own. "I don't mind being by myself."

"Are you sure, love?"

"Quite sure."

In the end Mrs. Tucker set off about half an hour before Willie and Marie were due back, and as soon as she had gone, Dan took off up the road to the training area to retrieve the two bags of loot they had been forced to leave behind when Willie got stuck in the cattle grid.

When he came to the dump, he found Ernest there, throwing spent bullets at a line of empty beer cans set up as targets. He seemed pleased to see Dan, and invited him to join in.

"Be more fun," he said, "a bit of competition, like."

"Why are you here?" Dan asked. "I mean, shouldn't you be doing something else?"

"Oh, sure to be," said Ernest, leisurely setting out the cans once more.

"If they want me, they can find me. I was told to empty this load of old cans, nothing else."

"I'd be afraid of missing something."

"Huh. Not much chance of that, worse luck. If they want you, they'll soon find you."

"Did you get to the enemy headquarters after we saw you?" Dan asked.

Ernest brightened. "Yeah," he said, "I did. My sergeant, he was surprised." He chuckled. "Less than half the platoon got in, and I was one of them. He couldn't get over it."

"You wouldn't have, if we hadn't helped you," Dan pointed out.

"Oh, aye. Where's your friend tonight, then? The one that's so clever with maps?"

"Willie? He's gone to a singing lesson."

"He's one of them kids that can do everything, is he? Must be nice to be like that."

Dan was so taken aback he could think of nothing to say for once, but just then Ted appeared over the brow of the hill.

"Thought you must have dropped off to sleep, mate," he remarked, then, seeing Dan, added, "Hello, you here again? Where's your pal?"

"Singing," said Ernest.

"Oh, yeah? Well, listen, mate, you'll have something to sing about if you don't look sharp. You're wanted for a briefing at headquarters."

"What did I tell you?" said Ernest to Dan. "If they want you, they'll find you."

"You don't need to sound so sore," said Ted. "It's something special, this is. It's only for those that did well on that field-course exercise, some sort of initiative test."

"Oh, yeah?" said Ernest, but he looked quite pleased and started to hurry back.

"I heard something about each of you picking a fellow to go

with you," Ted called after him. "So if it's something good,
don't forget me. And if it's something bad," he added, winking
at Dan, "forget me."

Dan thought Ted was a much brighter fellow than Ernest.
"It's not really fair," he said, "because you didn't have a chance
then. I bet you'd have got through if you'd been taking part."

"That's the army for you," said Ted. "How Ernie got by I'll
never know, but there's one thing I do know. He'll need someone with him who's got a bit more up top"—and he tapped his
head—"if he's going to get through the next caper they dream
up. Tell you what, mate. Have you got to be back within the
next half hour or so?"

"No," said Dan. "Why?"

"We're packing up and going back to base camp tonight to get ready for the real fun to start tomorrow afternoon, when this new exercise gets underway. Meantime I've got to drive around all the entry points and lower the warning flags, so that civilian vehicles know it's all right to go through. Would you like to come with me in the Land Rover?"

"You bet I would."

"Thought you might."

"Is it allowed?"

"Take a tip from me, son, if you're thinking of joining the army. Never go out of your way to ask if a thing's allowed. There's enough restrictions drummed into you without going around asking about things that nobody's thought to mention."

"If you're sure we won't get into trouble."

"None of the top brass are left up here, except our platoon commander. Just out of school he is; I'm none too bothered about him."

Dan thoroughly enjoyed the trip. There were more approaches to the ranges than he had realized, and since there was no one road going around the whole range they had to double back on their tracks a good many times to get around to them all.

When Ted drew up at the sixth warning flag, he said, "That's the last of them. Now, my quickest way back to camp is straight down the lane here to Penbont, but you live in the cottage at the foot of that other lane, don't you?"

"Willie does," said Dan. "I'm just visiting there."

"Same thing. I was just thinking. If you walked straight along this boundary fence you'd come back to where we started, about a mile down, and then it's no distance down the lane to your place. Be a lot quicker for me than having to take you all the way around by the road." He looked at his watch. "I'm a bit late as it is."

Dan agreed, hoping Marie wouldn't get upset if he wasn't home when she and Willie got back. "You're sure it isn't more than a mile?" he said.

"Sure," said Ted. "Look, I'll show you." He produced a map out of the glove compartment, and spread it out. The outline of the training area was marked in red ink, the roads in yellow, and it showed where all the flags were sited, and the small-arms range. Dan was fascinated by it. There were even little drawings of the human target figures, and the dummy tanks on their railway line. He noted the bridge under which he and Willie had hidden. On the map, the bridge and firing range looked no farther away than the cattle grid Dan had to aim for, but in a different direction. Dan looked up from the map to the landscape, and saw that a valley seemed to run straight and level in the direction of the firing range.

"Then it's only about a mile from here to the small-arms range," he said. "Is it straight up that valley?"

"Yeah," said Ted, looking at the map and then, like Dan, across the country. "You're sharp, you are. But don't you ever try going that way."

"I won't," said Dan. "If I don't hurry straight home, I'll be in trouble."

"That makes two of us," said Ted. "You keep right alongside that fence until you come to the cattle grid, then you can't go wrong."

Dan ran home as fast as he could, picking up the two packs as he passed below the refuse dump, and dropping them quietly in the garden shed before going into the house.

Marie was home, and was cross. She had hurried back with Willie only to find no sign of Dan. She kept saying to him, "But where have you *been*?" and when Dan told her truthfully that he had been driving around the army range with Ted she got even more cross. She kept on and on about its being very naughty of him to wander off on his own until Dan, tired of the continual nagging, told her she was stupid and bossy. Marie flounced off to the kitchen and heated up some baked beans, which she slammed down on the table, telling the boys to come and get it themselves, because she was going to take a bath.

The baked beans revived Dan's good temper. He told Willie about the map of the training area. "Tell you what," he said. "I'll draw it from memory, and then I can show you exactly where I went."

When the map was finished, they played a good game on it with the little plastic soldiers Dan had brought with him. It kept them happy until Mrs. Tucker and Shirley came home.

"There's good boys," said Auntie Ceinwen, seeing the peaceful scene. "Where's Marie?"

"In the bath," said Willie. "We've had our supper."

"Well, off to bed, the both of you, because you'll be having a late night tomorrow."

Instantly obedient, Dan cleared away his soldiers and folded his map, putting it carefully in his pocket. He wanted to be safely in bed and asleep before Marie came out of the bath.

8
The Eisteddfod

Next morning, which was Saturday, the Tuckers could think of nothing but the eisteddfod. Marie seemed to have forgotten about her fight with Dan, and he was careful not to say anything that might remind her of it. He was really looking forward to the eisteddfod himself, but realized it meant he might not have another chance to explore the training area. The next day was Sunday, and all the family would be at home, so he would not be able to slip off up there, and on Monday his father would be coming to fetch him.

That thought gave him a warm, comfortable feeling. He did not really mind about the training area because he had done just about everything it was possible to do. Now he could take lots of new ideas home to act out with his little soldiers on the familiar worn bedroom carpet. He had the map, too. He took it out and looked at it. When it was time to get ready to go he carefully transferred it to the pocket of his best pants, for Auntie Ceinwen had told him to leave his dirty clothes in the laundry basket for her to wash before he went home, and it would never do for his precious map to be reduced to pulp.

The eisteddfod started by being fun. They all set off for the chapel at the other end of Penbont, where it was being held, and crammed into a pew, with Willie at the edge, as he would be the first of the family to sing. There seemed to Dan a surprising number of other children all wanting to compete, but at last

Willie's turn came, and he sang his piece without any mishaps, looking unnaturally clean and brushed and wearing a shiny white shirt and blue bow tie. As soon as he returned he wanted to go off to the chapel vestry and get something to eat, but his mother made him wait until all the other competitors had finished and the judge had announced the results. When at last he got up to speak, Dan was much more nervous for Willie than Willie was for himself. However, the judge just said Willie had a good, true voice but lacked expression; and passed on to the next competitor. Dan felt it was a bit flat after all the preparation, but Willie was quite satisfied, and led Dan off to the vestry where stout ladies were serving sandwiches and cookies and cups of tea. Marie, whose turn would come later, came out with them to go to the toilet.

As the afternoon rolled gently on and faded into evening, the tidy chapel habits melted away. At first, everyone sat upright in their pews, the women in hats and gloves, the children with neatly brushed hair, and nobody spoke or fidgeted, but as the hours passed, all that changed. Children trotted up and down the pulpit steps to sing, followed by a few teenagers and then by all the adult competitors. The doors at the back swung ceaselessly to and fro as people came and went from music to food and back again. The pews became homes to the families who had set up house in them. The chapel was like a little world of its own.

Shirley and Marie sang their duet, and were placed third in their section. After that, Dan's interest waned. Willie had gone to sleep on his mother's shoulder and a girl friend of Marie had come to sit with her in place of Shirley, who had disappeared. Dan began to think the end must surely come soon, and he hoped Shirley would not be missing when it was the turn of the big choirs to compete.

"Shall I go and look for Shirley?" he asked Auntie Ceinwen. It would be a change from sitting still.

"If you like, dear," she replied. Marie's friend giggled. "I wouldn't bother, if I were you," she said.

Dan slipped out and wandered into the open air. Darkness had fallen since he had last been out, but the street lights lit up the grass and the pathway around the front of the chapel, and cast deep pools of darkness in the farther corners. Clusters of middle-aged men stood around, gossiping; the women were gossiping, too, but they were inside in the vestry. Dan could hear their voices drifting out above the clatter of dishes being washed, and folding tables being stacked away.

He wandered around the back of the chapel and found it full of young couples holding hands or talking softly in the darkness. A girl, leaning against the wall beside a youth, laughed, and though Dan could not see clearly enough to recognize faces, the laugh sounded like Shirley's. He decided that he was not really interested in finding her, and went back to the front of the building hurriedly.

Out in the town, the pubs had closed, and groups of Saturday-night revelers were making their way home. A few men went past, talking loudly, and then a group of youths and girls, all enjoying a joke. Behind them there came staggering along two men, one of them leaning heavily upon the other's shoulder, and breaking from time to time into snatches of song. Between songs they appeared to be having an argument.

Drunk, thought Dan delightedly, recognizing the symptoms from his television screen. He had never seen real-live drunks before, and watched the approach of the two men with interest.

It turned to disagreeable shock, however, when he suddenly recognized the pair, for they were in army uniform. It was Ted and Ernest.

Dan drew back, hurt and shamed. Drunkenness was funny in strangers, but somehow horrifying in someone you knew. If it had been Ernest who was the really tipsy one, it would not have been so bad, but it was Ted who was leaning heavily on his companion, singing and shouting at the top of his voice.

As they passed the chapel, he caught at the railings with one wild arm and pulled Ernest around to face the lighted window.

"Thass a pub!" he cried. "Told you there'd be another pub open somewhere, didn't I?" He wove his way unsteadily toward the gate, but Ernest tugged him away.

"That's not a pub, that's a church," he said. "I told you, it's past closing time."

"Course it's a pub!" cried Ted. "Lights, singing, crowds of people. Churches don't have that sort of thing in the middle of the night. You don't know nothing." He aimed for the entrance and would have fallen flat on his face if Ernest had not caught him.

"I wish I'd never asked you to come with me," he said, crossly.

"Now see here, mate," said Ted, "I'm not going to spoil my

Saturday night out to go mountaineering, not for no one."

"Oh, come *on*," said Ernest, wearily.

"Listen, Ernest ol' man, be a good fellow. We'll just have one more pint and then we'll go off up your mountain if you want. Hear all that singing?" The ladies' solo competition wafted out across the street. "They're having a lot of fun in there."

One of the men outside the chapel came over to the gate.

"Now see here," he said to Ernest, "you'd best take your pal back to camp, before he gets into trouble with the police."

"He ain't no pal of mine," said Ernest, bitterly.

"I only wants to buy a pint of beer," said Ted. "That's what pubs is for, isn't it?"

"The pubs are all shut and this is a chapel," said the man shortly. "You clear off back to camp."

Ted looked uncertainly about him. "All right," he said. "If you say so." He turned to Ernest. "If you want to go up that mountain, you'll just have to go by yourself. I've got to go back to camp. This gentleman says so."

Ted lurched off down the road, leaving Ernest hesitating by the gate. As he came to a road junction, he turned and waved. "I seen one!" he shouted. "There's a big blue light up here. I told you I'd find a pub open, didn't I?" He staggered off out of sight.

"That'll be the police-station light, no doubt," observed the man who had spoken before. "Maybe that's the best place for him. If I were you, laddie, I'd clear off back to camp. He's old enough to take care of himself."

The men looked at their watches and decided they had better go back into the chapel, for some of them were due to sing. Only Ernest and Dan remained behind, one each side of the railings. Dan did not know what to do, but the downhearted look on Ernest's face decided him.

"Ernest," he said softly, half hoping Ernest would not hear, but he turned at once and searched the darkness beyond the ring of light where he stood. "It's me," Dan went on, and came to the gateway.

Ernest looked at him without much surprise, and said, "How you do keep turning up when I'm in trouble."

"What's the matter?" asked Dan, though he felt he knew part of it.

"It's that initiative test," said Ernest. "You know, you heard him ask me to get him in on it. Well, I did, and look where it's landed me." He sighed a beery sigh, and Dan wondered how sober Ernest was himself. At least he could stand up and talk straight. Dan had been frightened of Ted in that state, but Ernest was not frightening at all.

"What happened?" Dan asked.

Ernest explained that in the initiative test they all had to pretend they were escaping prisoners-of-war, and make their way across country in pairs without being detected, and back up to the building by the small-arms range, where Dan and Willie had been landed in the truck on their first adventure in the training area. Ted had told Ernest that the best way to do it was to lie low until darkness fell and then set out over the hills, and that the best place to lie low was in a pub.

"So that's what we've been doing," Ernest ended. "Lots of pubs."

"But it's been dark for ages."

"I know. Once Ted gets a few drinks inside him, it's as if he can't stop."

"Why didn't you carry on without him?" asked Dan.

"We're meant to go together. Anyway, how am I supposed to find my way around these hills in the dark?"

"I know the way," said Dan, remembering the spot where Ted had put him down after they had driven around the ranges together. Ted had gotten out a map, and Dan had seen how the fence ran along in one direction for a mile, to the cattle grid which had been his way home, and how the lane had dropped down off the hill toward Penbont, where they were now, and that was about another mile. And he also remembered the straight and level valley between the hills running in the direction of the small-arms range, and that had been about a mile, too.

"It's a heck of a long way, I bet," said Ernest.

"Only two miles," said Dan. "Or about that, anyway." He remembered he had his map in his pocket, the one he had drawn from memory after seeing Ted's map, and he spread it out under the lamplight.

"Where did you get that from?" asked Ernest. Dan explained, and told him about his drive with Ted. Ernest studied the map for a long time. "There's no road that last bit," he said at length.

"It's very easy, though," said Dan. "And you'll be less likely to be seen. That lane"—he indicated the one leading down from the sixth flag place to Penbont—"it must come in somewhere down there." He pointed down the street, which led out of town from the chapel, beyond where Ted had turned off.

"Oh, yeah," said Ernest. "I seen that. Got signs at the bottom, same as on the one going up past your place. You know, Ministry of Defense vehicles, and that."

"That'll be it, then," said Dan. It was a beautiful moonlit night, and the chapel would be hot and stuffy. There was still sometime to go before the end of the eisteddfod, for all the big choirs were yet to perform. "I'll come with you part of the way."

They set off down the deserted road and soon reached the turning Ernest had seen. It was marked with army signs exactly like the ones by Willie's cottage.

"That's the one," said Dan.

They started up it together. Dan kept on going a little farther and a little farther, thinking they must surely be near the open hillside, until it seemed a pity, having come so far, to turn back. It was longer than he had thought, but at last the hedge came to an abrupt halt, and within a few yards they stood by the flag. They looked back over a vast landscape, silvered by the moon and speckled with peacock or amber beads wherever houses clustered thickly enough to have a row of street lamps. In between, the darkness was pricked by golden lights so small and scattered that Dan could only tell if they were houses or stars by their position, for the farther horizon melted away in a distant haze and he could not see where the land ended and the sky began.

The other way, ahead of them, the twin hills humped up black against the moon, and the strip of ground between them ran level and inviting straight into the heart of the training area just as it showed on the map.

"See?" said Dan. "You can't get lost, and it isn't any farther to the firing range than it is back to town. You'll be there before I get back to the chapel, almost."

"Thanks," said Ernest. He looked down at Dan. "You're a gutsy little devil," he remarked, a trace of admiration in his gloomy voice. "Aren't you scared of going down that lane by yourself?"

Dan was a bit, now he came to think about it, but there wasn't much to be done about that now.

"No," he said cheerfully. "What is there to be scared of? I won't get lost."

But when Ernest set off across the moor, his pack on his back, Dan felt very small and solitary beneath the moon. He ran down the lane as fast as he could go and never stopped until he came to the lighted street. Then he slowed down to get his breath back before entering the chapel.

The Penbont choir was just about to sing when he arrived. The conductor was standing with his back to the audience, his baton raised, as Dan slipped in, and he would not let his choir start until the creaking door had swung shut. Blushing, Dan slipped into the nearest vacant seat, and before very long, overcome by the warmth of the chapel and the lateness of the hour, he fell asleep on the shoulder of the elderly woman beside him.

He knew no more until he felt himself being lifted in somebody's arms. Opening bleary eyes, he realized the eisteddfod was over, and he was being carried out by the hotel driver, Alf, whom he had noticed singing in the Penbont choir.

"Did we win?" he murmured sleepily.

"Yes," said Alf. "We won all right. First prize."

Alf gave all the Tucker family a lift home in his car. As Dan staggered sleepily up the garden path in a daze of moonlight and music he remembered something.

"Willie," he said, "did anyone miss me while I was out?"

"Not that I know of," said Willie. "Where did you go? I didn't know you'd gone."

"I'll tell you later," said Dan, but he would have gone straight back to sleep as soon as he had crawled into bed if

Willie had not nudged him and said, "Where did you go, then?"

"Up on the mountain," he said. "Flag number six." He and Willie had numbered all the flags on Dan's map the day before when they had been playing soldiers.

"You never!" said Willie. "I don't believe it."

Sleepily, Dan told him about Ernest. For once Willie, who had slept longer at the eisteddfod, was the more alert of the two.

"Which flag's that, then?" he asked when Dan had finished.

"Look on the map," said Dan, yawning deeply. "In my pants pocket."

As Willie rootled and rustled, Dan sank toward sleep, but was jerked back when Willie said suddenly, "Where was he trying to get to?"

"The small-arms range," said Dan. "Now shut up. I'll tell you all about it in the morning."

Willie obediently climbed into their shared bed. Only when he was snuggled in under the bedclothes did he make another remark.

"I hope he doesn't fall into the marsh," he said.

9
A Dangerous Venture

"Marsh? What marsh?" said Dan, loud and clear. An interrupted snore from somewhere near made him open his eyes, and he saw that it was broad daylight. Dan craned his neck to see where the snoring came from, and there was Auntie Ceinwen lying flat on her back in the other bed, eyes closed, mouth wide open. The snores kept time with the rise and fall of the bedclothes.

Dan puzzled over the light and the snores for several half-awake minutes, for he could have sworn he had replied straight away to Willie. But it had been dark then, about two o'clock in the morning, and Auntie Ceinwen hadn't come upstairs to bed. Could a whole night have passed since Willie had mentioned the marsh?

Now, lying there with the sun slanting in through the tiny square window, Dan knew what marsh. A clear picture filled his mind of Willie running blindly out from behind the firing range to look for him, and squelching ankle-deep into boggy ground that stretched away, long and level between two hills, to a dip in the horizon. It was an area of tawny sedge, sprinkled with white blobs of cotton grass and splotched here and there with patches of emerald, that most treacherous of all mountain colors, for it is the color of all those plants that like to drop their roots down into bottomless mud.

Dan stirred uneasily in his bed. The marsh could be avoided, he told himself. Even Willie, running around in a blind panic, had stopped instinctively when his feet began to squelch into it. But that was in the daytime. In the color-draining moonlight, would anyone see the danger signs, or be able to tell where to turn to reach dry ground?

Perhaps there was no real marsh, just a patch of sticky ground at the far end, which Willie had run into. Dan rolled over and pulled the bedclothes around his ears. He could tell by the light that it was still quite early, and since everyone else was still sleeping after their late night, there was no reason for him to stay awake by himself.

Suddenly a remark of Ted's leaped into his mind. It was at the end of their drive around the training area, when Ted was showing Dan on the map how to take a shortcut home along the boundary fence. Dan had pointed out that the firing range lay only a mile away across the gap between the hills. Ted had said, yes, he was quite right; sharp, Dan was, very sharp.

Dan had not paid much attention to Ted's other remark at the time, but now in bed, the only one awake among that sleeping Sunday-morning household, the exact words echoed in his mind. "Don't you *ever* try going that way." Not, "Don't you try going that way," but "Don't you *ever* try going that way." It was a warning, not just for that occasion, not just a matter of not wasting time, but for all occasions.

Dan sat up, sick with panic. Auntie Ceinwen snored on. Willie stirred in his sleep, for Dan's upheaval had sent a cold draft down his back. Dan shook him, unable to bear his fears alone a moment longer.

As soon as Willie was awake, Dan laid a finger on his lips and said, "Willie, you must get up and come out on the landing. I've got something to tell you."

Willie rose up out of bed and followed him and said calmly, "Are we going to see if Ernest is stuck in the marsh?"

"Yeah," said Dan, taken aback. "How did you guess?"

"I talked about it, last thing," said Willie, as though the

whole course of events had been the most natural thing in the world.

They crept to the bathroom, which was conveniently downstairs, and put on their clothes from the day before, which Mrs. Tucker had told them to leave in the laundry basket ready for her to wash. Then they slipped out of the back door. As they passed through the kitchen Dan glanced at the clock and saw that it was ten to seven.

They scarcely spoke as they panted up the hill and turned right to follow the boundary fence along to the sixth flag. Everything up there was bright and normal and peaceful. The dew was sparkling in the early-morning sunshine and the mountain birds, pipits and wheatears, flipped away almost from under their feet as though nothing more alarming than the arrival of these two boys had occurred to startle them in this quiet place.

"Of course it will be all right, really," said Dan. "We're only going just so we needn't worry. We could go back to bed after, if we like. I bet they'll be still asleep when we get back."

Willie said nothing.

"Probably by daylight we'll see there isn't any real marsh at all," Dan went on, doggedly. "Or Ernest will have found it was getting boggy and gone along the side of the hill instead. The moon was very bright. At least, some of the time it was. I bet he got there before I was back at the chapel. Don't you think so?"

"Somewhere up here," said Willie, "they lost a three-ton truck in a swamp."

"Don't be crazy. They couldn't have."

"It got stuck, and they couldn't pull it out, so they left it and came back next day with a tow truck, and it had gone. Just sunk."

"Shut up," said Dan. "Anyway, I don't believe that."

"It's true."

"There's the flag," said Dan.

They rounded the fence and began to run across the level stretch of moorland between the hills. The turf was soaking wet from the dew, but the ground beneath it, though springy, was firm. There were places where the dark peaty soil showed between the clumps of grass, and if you stepped on them they were wet and your footprints made slimy patches, but they were easy to avoid.

Then the boys came to a patch of real marsh, marked by russet sedges and cotton grass. This was porridgy stuff. They worked their way around it, but saw that in order to keep on the good ground they were being led up a side valley instead of keeping along the main level way toward the firing range.

They stopped, and stared out over the marsh.

"Well, there's no one there, anyway," said Dan. Was that a good sign, or a bad one? When he had set out, it was simply to reassure himself, but now, since Willie's story about the three-ton truck, he did not find the empty marshland reassuring at all. He could see what Ted had meant. It was almost impossible to get to the firing range by this route. Fingers of marsh ran up all kinds of side valleys from the flag. No doubt one could work around each of them in turn but it would be easy to get lost in the process, especially at night. How much simpler it had looked, under the deceptive moon, to march straight up the wide corridor between the hills.

"What's that?" said Willie, pointing ahead.

"A rock," said Dan. There were several of them around, but this one, on closer inspection, looked a little different.

"A rock," said Dan, again, "or else a dead sheep."

"Or Ernest's pack," said Willie.

Dan stared at him, and back at the lump. It was gray-green, like a weathered rock, or wet sheep's wool, but there was an odd dark lump on top of it; the black face of the sheep's carcass, it could be, except that Welsh mountain sheep have white faces; or a crow perched on the rock, except it was too still, too lumpish, for that.

"Hey!" Dan shouted suddenly, at the top of his voice. "Hey!"

Unmistakably, the black lump moved, seemed to roll backward and give way to a whitish blur, then it dropped again.

Now there was no doubt. That lump was the head of a man, resting on something, the pack, probably; a man so far gone in exhaustion that he could neither wave nor shout, but only rear up his head for one despairing moment at the sound of children shouting, and let it drop back on his pack.

Dan found himself shaking all over. What should they do? The worst had not yet happened, but it still might, if they made the wrong decision. If they went forward to rescue him, they might fail. If they ran to get help, it might take ages, and by the time they got back, they might find . . . nothing.

"We ought to have brought a rope," said Willie. His matter-of-fact voice calmed Dan, and let his mind work properly again.

"There's a rope on the flagpole," he said. "We can untie the flag and pull the end down through the pulley. I'll get it—I can run faster."

They had not come very far, and now that Dan had been over the ground once, he was able to get back much more quickly. In five minutes he had untied the rope and was back. Willie had already set out across the marsh toward Ernest, carefully trying out each step as he went and Dan, by following in his footprints, was soon able to catch up with him.

At first the going was not too difficult, but soon it got much worse. The rope held between them gave them courage, however, and they pressed on over the quaking ground. Dan took the lead now, jumping across gaps from one tussock to the next that he would not have dared attempt had he not known Willie held the other end of the rope, and when it came to Willie's turn to follow, Dan could take his weight if he fell short, and pull him forward to safety.

Now Ernest was only twenty yards away, and had seen them. He raised his head and stared at them with terrible eyes set in a white mud-streaked face, and his mouth worked as though he was trying to say something, but no sound came out.

Dan came upon an oval of treacherous green moss, and

stopped. He noticed a great slide mark into it, and a muddy churned-up scar running through the moss and weed to where Ernest lay. This must be where he had slipped into the morass and struggled, half-sinking, half-wallowing, to where he now was.

Dan could not get to him that way, and looked for a possible route around. As he crawled cautiously along to the right, Ernest gave a great choked sigh and raised one arm above his head. At once, he sank lower into the bog, so low that he could no longer rest his head on the pack, and only by grasping it again with his hands could he save himself from sinking utterly.

"Hold on!" cried Dan. "We're coming as fast as we can."

"He wants you to throw him the rope," muttered Willie, seeing Ernest's eyes fixed on it, and guessing the reason for the upraised arm.

Dan thought about this. "I daren't," he said. "We must get around to the other side first." If he threw the rope now, and Ernest caught it, they would have to pull him the whole width of the morass, which they would not be strong enough to do, and if Ernest let go his hold on the pack, and missed the rope, he would sink at once.

As he wriggled on his stomach around the edge, he could see that all around him lay many more of the boggy pools, some topped with water, others greened over with moss and sundew. If Ernest had not fallen into that particular mire, there would have been plenty of others to engulf him. As Dan halfrose onto his feet to see how he could best approach the soldier, one leg sunk into ooze up to his thigh, and he flung himself back upon Willie, who hauled him out by the armpits.

With a slightly sick feeling, Dan wriggled on again, and Willie followed. Then they reached a patch of firmer ground, not really firm, but like stiffish porridge that has cooled and has a crust on top. A small willow grew there, its main stem no thicker than Dan's wrist, but it was something to hold on to. Dan decided he could grip the willow with one hand, and touch

Ernest with the other, but with success so
close, he dreaded doing anything rash.

"Ernest," he whispered, "you are not
to let go of your pack until I say so.
Understand?"

Ernest gave the ghost of a nod.

"You're too heavy for us to hold,"
said Willie. "We've got to get the rope
on you."

"Hold my legs," said Dan to Willie.
Willie grasped Dan's ankles and Dan,
taking hold of a willow branch with his
right hand, leaned out over the marsh and
tried to slip the rope's end under Ernest's
arms with his left. He could not reach,
though, and had to let go of the branch
and lie flat in the mud, plunging

both arms deep in the slime to get the rope under the soldier's body. He was very glad of Willie's firm grip on his ankles. The knot he tied at Ernest's back was a bungly affair, but he hoped it would hold.

"Put the other end around the tree trunk," he said to Willie, easing himself back onto firmer ground. "Under that bit of branch, so's it won't slip up over the top."

"How do I tie it?" said Willie.

Dan thought about that. He tried to work out in his mind how they could best use the little tree to help them. If the rope was tied to it as soon as Ernest got closer it would slacken, and not be any use. He thought how the rope on the flagpole ran through a pulley.

"Don't tie it at all," he said. "Just loop it round so that you can tighten it as we pull. Get it?"

"Yeah."

Dan looked along the length of rope, from Ernest, who seemed to be losing consciousness, across the yard or so of dark slime through which they had to pull him, to the more solid patch where the willow grew and Willie waited, solemn and safe, stocky as a young bull. There was nothing more to do in the way of preparation. He drew a long, shaky breath.

"When I say 'Pull,' we are going to pull you this way, on the rope," he said to Ernest. "You must let go of the pack, then, so we can pull you easier. Got that?"

Ernest seemed to be trying to say something, and Dan leaned out over the mud till his face was close to him.

"What did you say?" he asked.

Ernest's lips moved stiffly, and a husky sound came from his throat. "Good kids," he muttered.

"What did he say?" asked Willie, as Dan levered himself back.

"I'll tell you after," said Dan gruffly. "Okay, heave."

Nothing happened for a moment, then Ernest seemed to roll toward them. As he came, he slid lower and instead of letting go of his pack, he clutched it tighter in desperation. The rope, fastened low on the willow, helped pull him along, but did not lift him up enough, and he seemed to be sinking deeper and deeper.

Dan left the rope work to Willie, and seized Ernest by the collar. Ernest, in a panic, started to thrash about wildly. Willie, tugging away on the rope, felt the willow roots pulling out through the squelching mud, and stamped down with his feet where he could see the ground heaving.

The pack, wedged between Ernest and Dan, began to sink into the mud, and Ernest, feeling his last support going, scrambled desperately. His hands grasped Dan. First his knee and then his foot found the now-submerged pack, and he made a frantic bid for the bank.

For one instant Dan thought he was going to be pulled head first into the slime, but then he felt Willie's grasp on his jacket and the next minute the two of them lay sprawling on the safe ground. Ernest's legs still trailed in the ooze, and the boys pulled at him, trying to get a grip on the heavy body covered inches deep in black mud, until at last they had him lying safely beside them.

"Look," said Willie. The little tree lay uprooted on the ground. They were already resting on its branches, though they had been too absorbed to notice.

Ernest had collapsed after his flurry of exertion, and lay like a lifeless lump of slime, only the mud-streaked face and hands making him look human. The boys sat there for a while in silent, scared wonder. Willie was the first to speak.

"He's cold," he said. The morning sun shone down warm and bright, but it could not penetrate the thick coating of mud and reach the frozen body beneath.

"We'll have to get help," said Dan. "We could never get him from here by ourselves."

"We can't leave him alone," said Willie.

"No. One of us must go, and one stay." Dan did not want to part from Willie. He was strong, he did not panic, he asked the kind of questions that calmed Dan's whirling fears and made his mind work properly. All the same, Willie was right. Ernest made a feeble movement with one hand, and Willie patted him, like one would a frightened animal.

"You stay here with him," Dan said. "He likes you. Anyway, I can run faster."

He looked across the expanse of bog he would have to cross alone. This was not the sort of thing Captain Dan, that little figure in the corner of all Dan's army pictures, ever had to do. He only strutted around giving orders, arranging for aircraft to

be shot down, or enemies to be killed. But then, Captain Dan
would never have done anything so silly as to land one of his
men in a bog in the first place.

"Take the rope," said Willie. "If I keep hold of one end, it'll
reach for the hardest parts. It's quite long."

It made all the difference, that rope. It might not have been
much help if he *had* fallen in, but Dan felt much safer, and he
did not have to let go of it until he had got safely back around
that green morass.

"I'll be back as soon as I can," he shouted. "Don't let him try
to move, will you? Stay exactly where you are."

"Yes," said Willie. "All right."

Willie did not have long to wait. As Dan approached the
road, he could hear a vehicle coming up the lane, and he ran
forward just in time to stop it. The driver was the young officer
who was Ernest's platoon commander, and he had been out
looking for the missing soldier. Ted had already made a shame-
faced return from the police station.

What happened next all seemed incredibly quick and easy.
Dan spluttered out his story, the lieutenant spoke urgently into
his radio telephone, and in what seemed no time at all a helicopter was hovering over the marsh. Two men were winched
down on a line, and while one of them examined Ernest and
strapped him into some sort of stretcher, the other was hauled
back into the helicopter with Willie in his arms. Willie was
dumped on the bank where Dan stood with the platoon commander, and the helicopter returned to pick up Ernest and his
rescuer.

Suddenly Dan began, for the first time that morning, to look
ahead. When the helicopter had taken Ernest to the hospital, the
officer would have nothing to do but turn his attention to the two
boys who so mysteriously had known of his plight. Dan decided
he would rather not be around when the roar of the helicopter
had faded and questions could begin.

He pulled Willie by the arm, and backed away out of the officer's sight.

Still hanging on to Willie, he turned and ran back to the road, around the fence, and headed for home along the other side of it. Only when a clump of gorse hid them from the platoon commander did he allow Willie to stop and watch the helicopter winch up the two men and slide away up the valley.

"I wish I'd been winched up like that," said Dan. "What did it feel like?"

"I don't know," said Willie.

Dan stared at him. "You must know," he said. "Was it scary?"

"Yes," said Willie. "No, not really. I can't explain." He stared at Dan as though hoping Dan could understand how he felt just by looking at him, because he couldn't put it into words.

"Exciting?" said Dan.

Willie nodded. "It . . . it . . . it happened so quickly," he said at last.

Sometime, Dan thought, he must try and get more out of Willie, but in his heart of hearts he knew he never would. Meanwhile, there were other things to worry about.

"Come on," he said. "Let's go home."

"Why didn't we wait?" asked Willie.

"Better not. Your mom will be wondering where we are."

"Yeah," said Willie. "So she will."

10
A Visit from the Colonel

They were wrong. When they reached the cottage, wondering how they were going to get by in their filthy clothes if everyone was on the lookout for them, they found it as silent as when they had left—which was not quite silent, for standing beneath the open bedroom window they could still hear Auntie Ceinwen snoring.

"They can't all be asleep *now!*" whispered Dan. "What time is it?"

"No idea," said Willie. They tiptoed into the kitchen, where the clock hands pointed at half past eight. They stared at each other. It did not seem possible that so much could have happened and the day had not yet started.

"Let's take a bath," said Dan. Willie was surprised, because his bath time was always eight o'clock on Saturday evenings, but Dan pointed out that it was the only way to get clean enough to escape notice.

As the waterpipes did not go upstairs, they were able to bathe without much danger of disturbing the sleeping household. The real problem was getting the bathtub clean afterward. They dropped their dirty clothes back in the basket and put their pajamas on, and once in pajamas, the most sensible thing to do was to get back into bed.

Mrs. Tucker rose out of sleep just as they were climbing in, and assumed, not unnaturally, that they were just getting up.

"Woke up before me, have you?" she said, rolling over and yawning. She looked at her watch. "Dear me, I have slept on. It was that late night that did it. Fancy you being awake before me. You'll be needing another pair of pants, Willie. Don't go putting on your best ones."

Dan pulled on his clothes as fast as he could and fled downstairs and out into the garden.

By the gate he stopped and stood very still, listening for the approach of an army vehicle, and brooding. There had been no time to think before, and now, when he let his mind return to the morning's events, he felt sick and cold. More than anything, he wanted to be home, away from this stupid house, away from the training area—away, completely away from colonels and lieutenants and corporals and privates. He wanted to be at home, helping Dad train Biddy for the sheep-dog trials, or picking blackberries with his mom and Jean, or working with Jimmy among the clanking pails in the milking shed.

Suddenly he turned and ran indoors and halfway up the stairs. Then he slowed to a walk, strolled casually into the bedroom and picked up Ferdinand, trying to look as though he had really come for something else but might as well pick up the old donkey as he happened to be passing. Then he ran down and out to the garden gate again, where he stood, clasping Ferdinand to his chest, until Auntie Ceinwen called him in to breakfast. He tried to stuff Ferdinand into his pocket, but Ferdinand was too big, so he poked him under his shirt and came into the kitchen with arms folded, hoping the lump wouldn't show.

Willie ate solidly, but Dan was not hungry. "Too many sandwiches and cookies last night, sure to be," said Auntie Ceinwen.

Then the miracle happened, the wished-for thing that Dan could not have believed possible. A car drew up and Dan, peering out fearfully, saw not the dreaded army Land Rover, but his father's van.

He ran out and clutched his father.

"Hello," said Mr. Price, feeling the knobby lump under Dan's jersey. "What's Auntie Ceinwen been feeding you on?"

"Donkeys," said Dan, and pulled out Ferdinand. It was the kind of small joke he had been missing ever since he left home.

It turned out that the next day, when Dan's father should have been picking him up, he had been asked to help a neighbor with a farming job, so he had come a day early.

"I hope he's been behaving himself," he said to Mrs. Tucker over a cup of tea, while Dan scurried around collecting his things before Auntie Ceinwen should have a chance to discover the state some of his clothes were in.

"No trouble at all," Dan heard Auntie Ceinwen say, through the open door. "Except for the eisteddfod, they've not been out of sight of the house the whole week. Ever so good, he's been." Dan caught Willie's eye and, worried though he was, he managed to raise a small grin. Then the sense of gloom came over him again.

"I'm not taking those army things we got back with me," he said. "You can have them."

"Not the helmet?" said Willie.

"You can have them all, for all I care," said Dan.

"Thanks," said Willie. He looked hopefully at Dan's strained face. "Your dad says I can come and stay with you again next vacation. Can I?"

"Yeah, I suppose so," said Dan. He spoke unenthusiastically, for now there was no longer any reason for Willie's visits. All Dan wanted was to get away from every reminder of the training area as quickly as possible.

Then he looked at Willie, waiting humbly for a sign of welcome, and a whole lot of things about Willie came into his mind—Willie weeping in the cattle grid, Willie singing in the chapel pulpit, Willie in the scary marshes, steady as a rock, strong as a bull, brave as a lion.

"Yeah," said Dan, again. "You come. I'd like that."

Then he ran downstairs to the kitchen, where his father was still drinking his tea.

"I'm ready," he said. "Can we go now?"

When he had said his good-byes and thank-yous, and was in the van heading for home, his father glanced at him.

"You were in a bit of a hurry to leave," he said. "I thought you mightn't want to come home earlier than planned. Didn't you enjoy your visit much?"

"Oh, yes," said Dan. "I enjoyed it."

They drove for five miles in silence, and then Mr. Price said, "What did you do then, all week?"

"Nothing much."

"Bit dull, was it?"

"No."

At last they pulled into the familiar yard, and Dan got out of the van and walked carefully indoors, carrying his suitcase. His mother came out and hugged him. Jean and Jimmy were both away from the house.

Dan kissed her politely and walked upstairs, still carrying his case. He opened it, and took out Ferdinand. He sat on the bed a long time, not moving, although he heard his mother call his name twice. Then he heard his father come in and say, "Where's Dan got to, then?" His mother must have said something, because his father answered, "Very quiet—tired, most probably—seems they were up late at some eisteddfod last night."

He heard his mother coming upstairs. She stood in the doorway a moment, just looking at him as he sat there, quite still, holding Ferdinand. Then she came and sat on the bed beside him and said, "What's the matter, Dan?"

"Nothing," said Dan. "Nothing at all." Then he put his head down on her lap and cried.

He cried and he cried. For a long time his mother just sat there, holding him and saying nothing, waiting for the sobs to

pass. But there seemed no end to his tears.

"Tell me what's the matter, Dan," she said again. "You must tell me what's wrong." She led him downstairs and sat him on a chair by the kitchen fire and made him a hot drink, but still he went on crying.

"Tell me what's the matter," she kept saying, and every time Dan replied, "Nothing. Nothing at all."

She began to get angry. "Don't be silly, Dan; there must be something wrong. If you won't tell me, I can't do anything about it, can I?"

But Dan still wept. "Nobody can do anything about it."

Mrs. Price did not pay much attention when she heard a Land Rover come into the yard, thinking it was just a neighboring farmer come to see her husband. But then she realized Dan had stopped crying and was sitting very still. She got up and looked out of the window.

"Why, Dan," she said, thinking here was something to cheer him up if anything would, "it's an army vehicle, and there's two soldiers talking to your father. Come and see."

Dan shook his head and shrank back into the old armchair.

"I wonder what they want," said Mrs. Price brightly.

"Me," said Dan, and hid his face in the chair.

His mother stood looking at him in silence for a long moment, and then went over to the back door and opened it, in time to hear Mr. Price say, "You'd best come in and talk to the wife about it."

They came in, the older man introducing himself as Colonel Witherby, and the younger one as Mr. Willis. Dan, peeping out from the corner of the armchair, recognized him as Ernest's platoon commander, the one he had stopped on the road that morning. It was the same colonel who had pulled Willie out of the cattle grid.

"Get up, Dan," his mother muttered at him, a little sharply. Manners were manners, and it was not like Dan to let her down like this. "He's a bit upset this morning," she added to the colonel, by way of explanation. Dan climbed out of the chair and flattened himself limply against the wall.

The colonel looked him up and down. "Hero of the hour he may be," he remarked, "but he looks to me as though he ought to be in bed." He steered the unresisting Dan back into his chair. "You stay there," he said. "Shock, I expect. Delayed reaction."

"Hero?" said Mrs. Price. "What's he been up to, then? I thought from the way he's been acting he'd got himself into trouble."

"Depends on how you look at it," said the colonel. "Do you mind if we sit down?"

Mrs. Price led them through into the living room, embarrassed that she had needed to be asked. Mr. Price gathered up Dan and put him into a corner of the sofa beside him.

"Well, now," said the colonel to Dan. "What about telling us all about it?"

Dan shook his head dumbly. Then he whispered, "How is Ernest?"

"Ernest?" said the colonel.

"Private Plumb," said Mr. Willis.

"Oh, he's all right. Tucked up in the hospital sleeping it off. So you knew who he was?"

"Yes."

"And how he came to be in the marsh?"

"Yes."

So then Dan drew a deep breath and fixed his eyes on Ferdinand, whom he discovered he still had twisted around in his hands, and told them all about last night outside the chapel, and the ride around the moor with Ted, and the map, and quite a bit about the day they got carried away in the truck.

"What's this about a marsh?" asked Mr. Price. Dan fell silent. So it was the colonel who explained about the marsh, and Mr. Willis who told the story of the rescue, but there were parts of it that neither of them knew, and Dan found himself filling in little bits. "But how did you know to find me here?" he asked, at the end.

"We went to Willie's cottage first," said Mr. Willis. "They directed us on here."

"You shouldn't have gone out there," said Mrs. Price. "You and Willie. It was too dangerous."

"He could have disappeared," said Dan. "Like the three-ton truck. And it would have been all my fault."

"Ah," said the colonel. "Not so fast. You've broken a lot of army regulations capering about all over the training area, no doubt about it, but if Private Plumb is stupid enough to take his marching orders from a kid like you instead of following his proper army training, well, that's his fault."

Dan felt rather sorry for Ernest. "He wasn't very good at mapreading," he said.

"And you are, I suppose?"

"Ted said . . ." began Dan, and trailed away into silence.

"That map you made . . . have you still got it?"

Dan felt in his pocket and produced a crumpled piece of paper, folded very small. In the long pause while the colonel unraveled it, Mrs. Price said quietly, "It was very thoughtless of you, Dan. Taking Willie with you, too."

Dan said, "I couldn't have done it without Willie. I was much more scared than him."

"Willis," said the colonel, poring solemnly over Dan's map. "Fetch me that map from the Land Rover." He looked up at Dan. "Did you copy this direct, or do it afterward, from memory?"

"I did it afterward, so Willie and I could play with my plastic soldiers on it."

"It's a very good map, for *plastic* soldiers," said the colonel. "But there are some things you have left out. Thank you, Willis."

He took the military map and spread that out on the table, too. "You've got your flags and roads about right, and the small-arms range. But now, look. What are these things?" He jabbed a finger at the army map. "These tussocky shapes, along this valley. You know where that is, don't you?"

"Yes. Where Ernest fell into the marsh."

"Did you know what those shapes meant?"

"Grass, I thought."

"So you didn't bother to put them on your map. But you know now what they mean, don't you?"

"Yes," said Dan. "Marsh."

Colonel Witherby studied Dan's map again. "You need very fine pens to make a good map," he said. "Otherwise you have to draw things so big—like those targets, for instance—that they take up too much space and make all your distances come out wrong. And good strong paper that will take colored inks without smudging, and won't tear with constant use." Dan's map was already falling to pieces. "It's a good idea to trace maps, rather than copy them, only then you need proper tracing paper."

"Yes," said Dan, wondering where he was supposed to get all these things, and why the colonel was bothering to tell him about them.

"Willis," said the colonel. "When you get back, put in an order for a complete set of mapping equipment—pens, tracing grids, colored ink, map sheets, the works—and send them over to Dan here."

"For me?" said Dan. "Why for me?"

"To keep you busy and out of mischief."

"It's a present," said Mrs. Price. "Say thank you, Dan."

"Thank you," said Dan mechanically. "But I thought . . ."

"What did you think?"

Dan said nothing, so his father spoke for him.

"I reckon Dan thought you had come here to give him the father and mother of a scolding. Isn't that right, Dan?"

Dan nodded. Then he shook his head. "It wasn't just the scolding," he said. "It was what might have happened."

"Ah," said Colonel Witherby. "So long as you feel like that about it, you don't need a scolding. You've learned something. You won't make the mistake of thinking you know all the answers again in a hurry. Besides . . ." he paused, as though wondering how to go on. "We all make mistakes," he said.

"Not everybody has the guts to go and put them right afterward. What you and Willie did out there on the marsh was very frightening for you, and dangerous, and . . . what do you think about it, Willis? You were there."

"Very brave, sir. I wouldn't have gone out there to save my life. Anybody who walks out through that swamp to rescue somebody deserves a medal."

"A medal?" said the colonel, as though that were a new idea. "But then, of course, there might be questions asked about how Private Plumb got into the marsh in the first place. What do you think, Mr. Price?"

"I reckon a mapping set will do very well," said Dan's father. "He needs to be kept busy. But our Dan wasn't the only boy who went out to rescue the soldier. Young Willie went too, and he wasn't to blame for him being out there."

"I rather think Mr. Willis is fixing up something rather special in the way of a trip in the helicopter for young Willie," said the colonel.

"That's right, sir."

For a fleeting moment, Dan wondered whether he wouldn't rather have a trip in a helicopter than a mapping outfit, however splendid, but then he remembered that it was he, not Willie, who had nearly sent Ernest to his death, and it was Willie who had reminded him about the marsh. It would not be right for him to share in Willie's helicopter flight.

Mr. Price got up and put his hand on Dan's shoulder. "Well, if that's all settled," he said, "perhaps you'll excuse us. Dan and I have work to do out on the farm. Thank you very much for coming and telling us all about it."

Out in the yard, Dan turned to his father. "What work is that, then, Dad?" He was glad to be out on the farm again, free of the whole business, leaving his mother making tea indoors for the visitors, and no doubt talking everything over.

His father put his hand down to stroke the sheep dog that was curling around his legs. "Why," he said, "taking Biddy out with the sheep. The trials are next Saturday, remember?"